There was fire to her eyes now. Fire and spark. It was what he'd come to love about her. Hold on...

Love?

That was a strong word to describe his feelings.

"I had a choice just like everyone else. Bad things happen to good people all the time and whatever happens in childhood isn't a child's fault," Alice said, and he already knew he was in trouble with her. "But the day I turned eighteen, I figured that I had a choice about my life. I could blame my rough situation on everyone else and be miserable. Or I could take charge of my life and find happiness. Not that I'm all that great about that last part. I make mistakes, but I'm giving my best effort."

Alice stood toe-to-toe with him now. What she lacked in height she made up for in spirit.

"You didn't answer my question," he said. Staring into those blue eyes was like looking straight into the sun. He was going to get burned. He just didn't know how badly yet.

ONE TOUGH TEXAN

USA TODAY Bestselling Author

BARB HAN

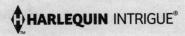

HARLEQUIN INTRIGUE®

I feel hugely blessed to be a Harlequin author. Working with my editor, Allison Lyons, is truly better than any gift I've unwrapped during the holidays. The same rings true for my agent, Jill Marsal. Thank you both!

Merry Christmas to Brandon, Jacob and Tori. I love all three of you. I hope you always know how very much!

The best present in my life has been you, Babe. Thank you for always encouraging me to follow my dreams and enjoying every step of the way as much as I do. With you, every day feels like Christmas. I love you!

ISBN-13: 978-0-373-75650-6

One Tough Texan

Copyright © 2016 by Barb Han

Recycling programs for this product may not exist in your area.

Printed in U.S.A.

USA TODAY bestselling author **Barb Han** lives in north Texas with her very own hero-worthy husband, three beautiful children, a spunky golden retriever/standard poodle mix and too many books in her to-read pile. In her downtime, she plays video games and spends much of her time on or around a basketball court. She loves interacting with readers and is grateful for their support. You can reach her at barbhan.com.

CAST OF CHARACTERS

Alice Green—Guilt forces this cop to go rogue and put everything on the line to locate a kidnapped teen. Her unsanctioned action leads her to one of the most wanted criminals in the United States and causes her to interfere with an FBI investigation. But the biggest risk might be the handsome cowboy who threatens so much more.

Joshua O'Brien—This cop on temporary leave is the youngest of the six O'Brien brothers (and a twin) by two minutes. He's planning a future with the FBI until a woman in trouble comes along who could jeopardize his heart and destroy his career in the process.

Isabel Guillermo—A kidnapped teen Alice is willing to risk everything in order to save.

Erin Daily—A young girl who might have information that could lead Alice to Isabel.

Ryder O'Brien—This twin will always be there for his brother, even if it means risking his own life.

Tommy Johnson—The sheriff who grew up at the O'Brien ranch and considers them family.

Special Agent Fischer—The FBI agent who walked away from Alice, and fatherhood, seems to have had a change of heart. Will he stand in the way of her investigation and her life or step down when the time comes?

Marco Perez, aka The Ghost—One of the most wanted and ruthless men in America is known for erasing anyone outside of his organization who has ever seen him.

Bill and Kelly Harding—Isabel's foster parents don't seem terribly upset that she has disappeared.

Chapter One

Joshua O'Brien eased his foot off the gas pedal. His Jeep shuddered before the power died. He was out of gas in a flash flood thirty miles from the family ranch in Bluff, Texas. He cursed his floating gas gauge as he pushed open the driver's side door. Running two towns over to Harlan to pick up a box of donations to be auctioned off at his family's annual Christmas Benefit wasn't exactly his idea of an exciting Friday night. When the Nelson widow had opened the door in her red silk bathrobe and then offered him a nightcap, he'd been even less thrilled. Drawing the short straw to make that pickup—and deal with the seventy-year-old Mrs. Nelson—was just one in a long list of reasons that Joshua wasn't cut out for the family business at the Longhorn Cattlemen Ranch and Rifleman's Club and it made him miss his job in law enforcement that much more. Could he make his temporary leave permanent in order to stay on at the ranch? The decision could wait.

He shook off his bad luck, grabbed a gas container from the back and trudged through the ankle-deep water. According to his phone's GPS, there should be a gas station a few blocks ahead. He figured he could walk there and back quicker than one of his brothers could drive into town from the ranch to get him so he set out on foot rather than make a call for help and admit his own stupidity.

It was the kind of pitch-black night outside that made it hard to see much past the end of his nose. His eyes would adjust in a few minutes. A bolt of lightning raced sideways across the sky, emphasizing layers of thick gray clouds as far as he could see. This storm wasn't passing anytime soon. Joshua checked his surroundings. He'd passed the quarter acre cul-de-sac lots and was now walking past a field with overgrown grass. The bad weather must be keeping everyone indoors because the roads were empty. That meant no chance of hitching a ride.

A flash flood alert had already buzzed on his cell. If he hadn't been distracted thinking about his parents' murder investigation then he would've filled up the tank sooner, instead of sloshing through water that was rapidly gathering on the roads and sidewalks while wearing his good boots.

He still couldn't think of a soul who'd want to harm his folks. His father, a self-made millionaire cattle rancher who'd owned a few thousand acres in Bluff, Texas, had built his business on handshakes and hard work. His mother, the matriarch of the family, was as kind as she was giving. Joshua and his five brothers had inherited the lion's share of the family business, which included a successful rifleman's club. A token share went to their aunt and uncle, same as it had been when his parents were alive. The brothers had voted to give a devoted worker a piece of the pie.

Joshua's investigation experience told him to look at those who were closest to his parents, the ones who had the most to gain. Skills honed by Denver PD told him to look for motive, means and opportunity. The only people who stood to benefit from his parents' murders were him and his brothers. None of his brothers had motive. Each was successful in his own right and the O'Briens had always been a loving, close-knit bunch. It couldn't be one of them, which led Joshua to believe that someone had a beef with his parents. It was the only thing that made sense. And he drew a blank there, too. There were no secret affairs, no emotional dramas with friends. His parents were exactly as they appeared on the surface. Generous. Kind. Loving.

The sheriff was checking every angle. He was a close family friend and Joshua knew he was taking the news just as hard.

A warm glow, most likely a streetlight in the distance, meant Joshua was getting closer to the station. At least it wasn't freezing cold outside like it had been recently. Christmas was three weeks away and weather this time of year was unpredictable.

Another bolt of lightning helped Joshua see that if he cut through the field he'd get to the station faster. He took a step onto the land and knee-deep grass. Heavy rain. Tall grass. Horrible luck. Looking down caused water to run off the rim of his Stetson, but he didn't care. His eyes were beginning to adjust to the darkness, which meant he'd been on foot for a solid fifteen minutes already. The station was ahead and he stepped up his pace through the field. As he made the clearing he noticed a teen, maybe sixteen years old based on her petite build, walking ahead of him. Was someone else stranded in this crazy weather?

She seemed a little young to be out walking on a night like this. He started to call out to her when a flash of lightning blazed across the sky and he caught sight of a man watching her intently from behind the trash bins of the gas station. Thunder rumbled in the distance and Joshua counted three seconds in between the flash and the noise. That meant lightning was right on top of them.

Joshua's pulse spiked as he spotted another man crouching at the edge of the field as the unsuspecting teen kept bebopping along. She must have no idea the amount of danger she was about to walk into. And Joshua didn't either because he counted a third man closing in on her from the east. How many others were there?

Based on the way she made the occasional stop to shake her arms or perform some other dance move, Joshua figured that she must be wearing earbuds. That wasn't her brightest move for a couple of reasons. For one, she didn't need to be wearing electronics in a storm. For another, it meant she wouldn't hear him even if he screamed at the top of his lungs. That would, however, alert the men bearing down on her like hunters closing in on a quarry.

Damn, his shotgun was locked inside his Jeep.

Dropping to crouching position, Joshua tried to make himself as small as possible—not exactly easy with his six-foot-four-inch frame—

as he shifted all his attention to the teen. She kept her head down. She was wearing jeans that were plastered to her legs and a couple layers of tank tops slick from rain.

And she had no idea what was about to go down.

The big question was how Joshua was going to get her out of this mess. Staying low was his best chance of not being noticed. He palmed his cell, moving closer. Could he call his friend Tommy Johnson, the sheriff? Probably not without being seen. The light from his phone could give him away. If the men saw him, he had no idea what they were capable of doing to him and the girl. Then again, an ill-timed bolt of lightning would have the same effect.

His Jeep was too far away to run back and get his shotgun. The men would be long gone with the girl. He focused on the teen as he moved closer to the gas station. She had a tiny frame and hair for days that she was trying to wrangle into a ponytail. Even wet he could see how thick it was. With her back turned, Joshua couldn't see the details of her face, but the rest of her looked straight out of an Abercrombie & Fitch ad. Scanning the area, watching the men, Joshua knew that this was a coordinated kidnapping attempt. Outnumbered by at least three to one, Joshua calculated the odds of getting to her and they weren't good.

Could he use the darkness to cloak them both? One wrong move and he'd be exposed. She wouldn't have a chance on her own. He needed a plan and yet there was no time to make one. If the men got to her first it would be all over. No way could he handle three against one without a weapon of his own. He'd turned in his service weapon and had stopped carrying his backup since he spent most of his time with cattle on the ranch.

Joshua glanced down at the gas container in his hand, sloshing around what little leftover contents were at the bottom. There hadn't been enough to get him to the gas station, but there might be enough to create a diversion. Distract the men for a few seconds and grab the teen. If he could get her into the convenience store safely there'd be shelter and witnesses. That should scare these guys off. He hoped.

Joshua tucked away his cell and then fished his emergency lighter from the front pocket of his denim jacket. With all this water coming down everywhere, he needed something that he could use as a wick. Nothing was dry.

Lighting the plastic container on fire right next to him was too much of a risk. He cleared an area, poured a little of the gasoline out and then rolled several times until he was a few feet from the container.

Joshua flicked his lighter and then tossed it toward the spot. He didn't wait for it to light up, he bolted toward the teenager.

As the blaze ignited, Joshua wrapped an arm around her waist.

Maybe it was fear that had her frozen but he'd expected a fight. He noted that her struggle was weak at best. Shouldn't she be biting and kicking to get away? Other than a little squirming, she wasn't doing much to help herself. Joshua was even more grateful that he was there to help.

He sprinted toward the gas station. Lightning struck as he scrambled onto the lot, illuminating the man by the trash bins. Joshua could see the guy's face clearly and the dude was looking right at Joshua. Not only was his gaze fixed, but he made a move toward a weapon, a gun maybe, as Joshua barreled around the corner, memorizing the details of the guy's face in the light. He had black-as-night hair, and an oval-shaped face. His eyes were set wide and his nose prominent. His eyebrows were bushy, his forehead large and he had a decent amount of scruff on his chin. His face was familiar but Joshua couldn't place it.

Then he heard someone cussing at him, realized it was coming from the teen as she started actually fighting. Good for her.

"You're okay. I'm not going to hurt you," Joshua said, trying to reassure her. She must be confused and scared as he rounded the corner.

"I didn't think you were, jerk," she shot back.

What the...? Not the reaction he was expecting but then she was probably still in shock.

"Put me down," she demanded. Her voice was a study in calm.

"Not so fast," he said, scrambling inside the station.

Her response came in the form of twists and turns so quick he almost lost his grip around her tiny waist. Her elbow slammed into his ribs. Did she want to be taken by those scumbags?

"Call nine-one-one," Joshua managed to say to the attendant as he shot down an aisle, trying to recover from the blow and stay on his feet. His law enforcement training had kicked in and adrenaline was on full-tilt. He'd lock them in the bathroom until help arrived.

Joshua managed to open the door to the men's room even though the teen was fighting him like a wild banshee. Her freeze response sure made a wide turn into fight mode in a hurry.

"Cut it out. I'm trying to help, if you hadn't

noticed," he said through heavy breaths. She wasn't making it easy, either.

He stuffed her inside the bathroom with him and then locked the door. "Those men weren't exactly trying to take you to prom."

Joshua heard a familiar noise and realized he shouldn't have turned his back on her. He whirled around. There she stood. A Glock aimed at the center of his chest.

Now didn't that just make this night even better?

"What do you think you're doing?" he asked, noticing how off his initial assessment of the teen, the woman, had been. Strips of hair clung to her neck even though most of her blond mane was in a ponytail. She had piercing crystal-blue eyes—eyes that shone like he was looking across the surface of Diamondhead Lake at first light—and she had thick, dark lashes. Her body had more curves than he'd initially realized; he'd felt those the second he'd picked her up. They were easier to ignore when he thought she was sixteen. She was closer to his age, so around thirty and his throat went dry despite water dripping from him everywhere.

She was soaked, crown to toe, and as much as Joshua didn't like it, he felt a surge of attraction. All of which was overridden by the anger coursing through him. Even though she put up a good fight, he disarmed her quickly and then wrestled her against the wall before she could make a dive for her weapon that he'd sent sprawling across the floor.

His body had that same irritating sexual reaction when it was pressed up against hers. He captured her wrist as she nailed him in the chest and then he caught her other as it rose up in a fist. He pinned both of her hands above her head. Big mistake, a) because the move caused her breasts to rise and press against his chest harder, and b) because her knee shot up quickly.

Joshua pinned her thigh with his before she could knee him where no man wanted to be kneed.

"What's your problem, lady?" he asked, staring into furious blue eyes.

"BACK OFF. YOU HAVE no idea what you've gotten yourself into," Alice Green said, fuming that this guy had disarmed her so quickly. She was exhausted and getting rusty now that she'd been off the job for the past six weeks, having dedicated herself solely to finding Isabel. "And let go of me."

The cowboy might be the epitome of tall, gorgeous and chivalrous but his good deed had just cost her the investigation. Alice cursed.

This was the closest she'd been to Marco

Perez, aka The Ghost, in days. She'd spent long weeks before that researching crime rings to narrow it down this far, and had been abducted by two other criminal organizations. The last time she'd seen her boys was Thanksgiving Day. Since then, she'd been choked, punched and stabbed. And it had come down to The Ghost as her last chance to find Isabel.

Alice had put herself out there as bait, using her informant to plant the seed and set up the kidnapping. It had been difficult undercover work and had taken more patience than she realized she had. Perez's organization finally bit and this jerk had just messed up weeks of damn fine police work in sixty seconds. Well, if she'd still been on the force.

Alice was furious. And frustrated. And she could think of another word she'd like to drop when it came to the cowboy's actions but it wouldn't do any good. The fact that he was acting on goodwill was the only reason she didn't completely unleash hell on him.

"I have to go," she managed to get out through clenched teeth. If the task force found out what she was up to after being warned to stay away she'd lose everything, including her twin boys. "Thanks for going all Dudley Do-Right on me but I need to follow those men out there."

Tall, Dark and Cowboy cocked an eyebrow. "I'm sure the police would be happy to help as soon as they get here."

"I don't have time to lose," she countered. "They're getting away as we speak."

"Then tell me what's going on and I'll consider letting up," he said, staring her straight in the eye.

She ignored the shiver racing up her arms, chalking up her goose bumps to being soaked to the bone in an air conditioned bathroom. Didn't the worker believe in turning on the heat?

Telling the truth wasn't an option. Fighting didn't help. She'd have to take another approach.

Alice relaxed her body against the strong cowboy, looking up at him with her most sincere expression as she prepared a lie. "I'm sorry. Thank you for helping me. I don't know what I would've done if you hadn't been there. That guy out there is my ex and I really need to know what he's up to for the sake of our boys."

Shock registered in the cowboy's eyes. He had a rare combination of green eyes and black hair—no, black wasn't a good enough word—it was more like onyx.

Water dripped from his thick black eyelashes

and his tight curls. She could tell that he'd been wearing a hat, and in this part of the country that meant a Stetson. He was tall, six feet four inches would be her best guess. Based on the ripples running down his chest, she'd say the guy spent serious time at the gym. His hands were rough, which meant he worked outside. But not too rough, telling her that he hadn't been doing it for long.

"Are you telling me you know that guy?" he asked and she could tell he wasn't buying her story.

"Intimately." It was easy to sell that last part because it was the truth. Alice did know more details about Marco Perez's life than she ever wanted to about any criminal on the loose. He was the head of a large-scale kidnapping ring known for selling teenage girls or using them for baby farms. He was also most likely long gone by now. His ability to disappear and make every witness around him do the same had earned him The Ghost moniker.

Alice couldn't afford to explain herself to law enforcement. They'd run her name and she'd be discovered. She had to protect her identity.

"What's your name?" she asked. If she could bait this guy into casual conversation she had a chance at making it out of there before the cops arrived. With her arms hauled over her head the cowboy was in the power position.

"Joshua O'Brien," he said. "Now it's your turn."

It was a statement, not a question and she figured that she was grossly underestimating this guy.

"Will you let me go if I tell you, Joshua?" She'd used his name on purpose. Get him talking, get him comfortable and she could break out of his grasp.

"Maybe," he said.

"I'm Alice," she responded. The cops would be banging on that door in a matter of minutes in a best-case scenario…a matter of seconds in her worst nightmare. In no way could Alice allow that to happen. She'd be taken to jail and her reputation, as well as her career, would be over. As it was she could still return to the force after she located Isabel and brought her home safely.

Sirens wailed in the distance, which meant cops were getting closer. She needed to move faster with the cowboy in order to get away. Or distract him long enough to…

The chance presented itself, so she took it.

The cowboy had loosened his grip. Alice drew her knee up and tagged him as hard as she could in the groin.

She dropped and spun, breaking free from his grasp. A sweep of her right leg and he stumbled to catch himself.

He recovered quickly using the wall to redirect his weight, but he wasn't fast enough.

Alice pulled her backup weapon, a Glock G42 .380 pocket pistol, from her ankle holster. "Hands where I can see 'em, cowboy."

He righted himself and complied.

Now all she had to do was walk out that door and never look back. She made a move toward it and then stopped, a bout of conscience eating at her. It was her fault that the cowboy was in this mess. He'd seen Perez. Worse yet, The Ghost had seen the cowboy.

No one lived who could describe Perez. He was one of the most ruthless criminals in the country and he protected his identity with the ferocity of a starved lion.

But how could Alice protect her own identity and spare the cowboy's life?

Chapter Two

Alice's voice was high-pitched and had that listen-up-or-I'll-shoot quality. The attitude registered with Joshua as law enforcement. Was she on the job? Alice had that same swagger he'd seen in the officers he knew; granted hers was a heck of a lot sexier than theirs. Based on her reactions so far she was covering something—something big. She wasn't breaking the law, or at least not currently, so he was even more confused by the fact that she was adamant about not bringing in the police. He figured this wasn't the time to tell her about his law enforcement background or the fact that he had an application in at the FBI—a fact he hadn't shared with his brothers yet. He shoved the guilty feeling aside. He'd deal with that later.

"I'm running out of time. Word of advice. Forget what I look like," she barked. "And forget all the details about tonight."

Joshua put his hands up, palms flat, in surrender mode. "Sorry. Too late for that. But it's not for you. You haven't done anything wrong."

She shot him another look that told him he didn't have a clue.

"I'm serious about this next part so listen up. When the law arrives, tell them that you're being hunted by Marco Perez. Do you hear me?" she asked with seriousness in her voice that left no room for question.

He nodded, keeping watch on her and the door while tamping down his reaction to the name she'd just thrown out. The name Marco Perez was on every watch list and that's why his face had looked familiar.

"Also, and I can't stress this next part enough, you need to surrender to protective custody. Tell the sheriff what I said about seeing Perez and he'll arrange everything."

"We can talk this through and get help for you." Joshua wasn't ready to tip his hand about his own background, especially since she hadn't figured him out.

She shook her head.

"This whole situation can be sorted out. You don't have to keep running. Nothing is as bad as it seems," he added, trying to stall. She was the one who needed protection and most likely a skilled attorney.

"I know he saw you," she said, backing toward the door, keeping her intense gaze on him. "And he'll come back for you. Mark my words. No one who has ever seen Perez in action has lived to tell about it."

"Whatever it is you think you need to do... don't," Joshua said. He didn't need to be reminded of that rumor about Perez. His gaze bounced from the gun that had been tossed onto the floor to her again. He'd protect himself from Perez. Who did she have?

She made a move to open the door, keeping a close eye on him.

Joshua had no plans to be shot in the men's room of a gas station. That wasn't even a good cliché.

"Hold on," he said, trying out that same authoritative voice she'd used on him a few minutes ago. It was his cop voice.

Her gaze kept bouncing from him to the door, and instincts honed from years of police work told him she was about to flee. Given that she was obviously in some kind of trouble, even though she seemed more concerned about him at the moment, he needed to act fast or she'd disappear and he couldn't help her. Joshua held out his wrists. "Fine. You win. Take me into protective custody."

She balked.

"You need someone in law enforcement to do that," she said in that crisp, do-as-I-say-and-don't-ask-why voice and he'd be darned if it didn't sound sexy coming from her. With everything going on around them he shouldn't even notice. Being turned on by a woman who'd pulled a gun on him twice now wasn't his brightest move.

Then again, she was beautiful and his body reacted with a mind of its own. Logic had nothing to do with it.

"You're right about that. I do need someone in law enforcement to put me in protective custody." He didn't budge. "And since your cover is blown, it might as well be you."

The only thing he couldn't figure out was why she wasn't coming clean about being on the job. Best he could figure she'd been on some kind of detail, which made more sense as to why she fought when she did earlier. Was she in the middle of an undercover operation? Then again, if she was wouldn't she want police protection now?

Not necessarily. If she was in deep, she'd want to stay that way. Before he could raise another argument, she slipped out the door. He immediately bolted toward it but she'd managed to secure it with something on the other side.

Joshua muttered a curse as he pulled out

his cell. Explaining this whole scenario to his friend Tommy ensured that he'd be ribbed about this forever. He'd allowed himself to be locked inside a bathroom while the "teen" he'd been trying to save got away.

Best case scenario? Tommy was already pulling up in front of the gas station. The door opened at the same time Tommy's line rang.

"Turn that thing off." The mystery woman had returned. The business end of her gun pointed squarely at his chest. "And my name's Alice Green."

"If you're running from the law, it wasn't your best move to come back," Joshua said flatly.

"I know that. So, don't make me regret it." There was something else in her eyes this time. Fear?

Curious, Joshua ended the call. He didn't know what she'd gotten herself into but preferring a murderous criminal's company to the sheriff's didn't signal good things about her head being on straight.

"You have to decide right now," she said, her gaze bouncing from him to the hallway leading to the store as the sound of sirens moved closer.

He didn't budge.

"Please." There was a desperate quality in her eyes that tugged at his heart. She could've shot him twice now and hadn't so he figured she wasn't planning to hurt him. And he was more than mildly curious what she was really up to.

"Okay. But you're going to tell me what this is about," he said, bending over to retrieve the weapon they'd discarded earlier.

"Don't even think about it," she said as he made a motion to pick it up.

"I leave it here and they finger you immediately." If it was her service weapon then they could trace the serial number. Joshua at least wanted to hear what she had to say before he hauled her in to Tommy. He might even be able to convince her to turn herself in and that would make things a lot easier on her legally. But then, she would already know that.

"Where are we going?" he asked.

"Do you live nearby or have a ride anywhere around here?" She kept a brisk pace as round two of pouring rain flooded them.

"Yeah, my Jeep's a couple blocks away. But it won't do any good."

"Why not?" she asked, navigating them out of the dark parking lot as the sound of sirens neared.

Either she or Perez had shot the light out in back of the convenience store and his money was on her. "Out of gas."

She muttered a curse as she led him into the field.

"Stay low," she directed.

"You know that clerk can give the police our descriptions," Joshua hedged.

"He was too surprised to pay attention. He won't be able to give them anything more than a general idea. You're tall and that might mean something outside of Texas but all the men seem over six feet here. Plus, we rushed in and straight to the back without showing our faces. No way will that young kid be able to give them anything they can work with and any recording will be too grainy to make out," she responded matter-of-factly.

More proof that she knew a little too much about the process to hold up her claim of not being in law enforcement. Plus, he picked up on the fact that she was from out of state because of her height reference. No one in Texas really thought about whether or not six feet was tall.

"Why are you running?" Joshua asked.

"I'm not," she dismissed him.

"Maybe the appropriate question is, Who are you running from?" It couldn't be Perez since she was trying to be captured by him. She'd said they had boys together, another reason he should ignore any sexual current flowing between them. Once they were safe he'd ask her about her family situation.

"Stay down and be quiet if you want to get out of here alive," she said, irritation lining her tone.

Since Alice, if that was her name, was already belly down he figured he'd better do the same. She'd holstered her weapon and that reminded him of the fact she wore an ankle holster in the first place. No one did that outside law enforcement.

"Where are you from?" he asked.

"Tucson," she said.

"Why are you really here?" he asked, retrieving his hat.

"I already told you," she said. "My ex."

"You can drop the act," Joshua said, not bothering to hide the fact he was done with lies. Besides, the thought of her returning for an ex stirred a different reaction inside him—jealousy? "Nobody and especially not me believes you came all the way out here to be abducted by the father of your children."

He intended to find out what she was really up to and how much of what she'd said was the truth.

WAITING FOR OFFICERS to clear out of the gas station while lying belly down in two inches of water wasn't Alice's idea of a great Friday night. Then again, being dumped by the father of her twins two weeks before the babies had arrived hadn't been, either. Fridays were right up there with poking her eyes with hot sticks.

Soaked to the bone, she shivered as she waited for the cruiser to leave the gas station. The cold front that had been promised was moving in. Experience told her that the clerk hadn't actually witnessed a crime so there wouldn't be much to investigate. A deputy would take a statement, file a report and move on. Then, he or she would keep an eye out for anything suspicious in the area for the rest of the night.

The deputy left ten minutes after he'd arrived.

"Take my jacket," Joshua said, sitting up, water sloshing as it rolled off him and hit the puddle on the ground.

"It's okay. I can handle it," she said quickly. Being on the force, Alice had learned not to admit weakness. Officers depended on one another in life-threatening situations and being a woman she felt that she had to prove herself even more so than male officers. Men had a height and weight advantage, and they tended to be stronger. Alice wasn't the tallest person at five feet four inches and she'd been mistaken for a teenager by people approaching from behind more than once while wearing street clothes. She'd had to work hard to compensate for her size differential.

"Your teeth are chattering," the cowboy said. And his tone almost made her laugh out loud. He sounded almost offended that she hadn't accepted his chivalry.

A female cop coming off as needy or not being able to pull her weight killed her career before it got started. It was a certain way to make the officer next to her wonder if she could come through in a clutch and since lives were at stake everyone took that seriously. So, even if it made her look stupid or she caught the death of a cold later she couldn't accept his jacket.

"Believe it or not, I can take care of myself and I have been for a long time. I don't need your charity," she quipped defensively. Spending time with this cowboy was going to be fun. If by fun she meant stabbing her fingers with a serrated knife.

"Suit yourself," came out about as flat as her pancakes.

Hey, it was the twenty-first century. Women weren't slaves to the kitchen anymore. And that was pretty much how she defended her lack of cooking skills. She could, however, make one mean pot of coffee. And wasn't that more important anyway? "The gas container you used to create a diversion earlier should be around here somewhere."

"Yep."

Great, now they were at one-word answers. She'd spent enough time around the opposite sex to know that she'd offended him, didn't have time to care. He was alive. He could thank her later. "Think you can find it?"

"Of course."

At least he was up to two words now.

Maybe she should've left him back at the station. Except that she was responsible for getting him into this mess in the first place and she couldn't let him get himself killed given that he was genuinely trying to help her. And stupidity could be deadly.

Joshua was a liability.

She needed to convince him just how much danger he was in and that he needed to turn himself in. There was a reason she'd saved Perez's organization for last. People didn't walk away after they saw him. He had no qualms about erasing a threat, real or perceived. Precisely the reason he was considered one of, if not *the* most ruthless criminal in the United States.

It was getting late. The trail was a dead end now. Alice was starving and she needed to get back to her motel room to bunk down for the night while she came up with plan B. She also needed to touch base with her informant and let him know everything had gone south.

Pushing up to her feet proved more of a challenge than she expected. She landed down on her bottom pretty darn quick with a splash.

The cowboy was by her side in a half second, helping her to her feet.

"I haven't slept in a few days," she said quickly and a little too sharply.

"Yeah? Even Superwoman needs rest."

She didn't say anything and the cowboy didn't budge.

"When was the last time you had a decent meal?" he asked, standing so close that her body was aware of his every breath.

"It's been a while. I got distracted tracking this lead," she quipped. Exhaustion was taking a toll and she couldn't help herself. Her tone tended toward being harsh in a situation like this. "Thanks for the hand up, by the way."

"No problem. You don't have to sound like I broke your arm."

What? Did she? Okay, that did make her feel bad. She wasn't trying to be a jerk.

The cowboy chuckled as he turned and walked away.

Oh, so he had a sense of humor. Under different circumstances, Alice might actually laugh. Searching for Isabel nonstop for the past six weeks had brought her to the brink of exhaustion. Then there were the twins. Two baby boys who had one speed…blazing. She missed her boys so fiercely it had physically hurt since she'd left home three weeks ago on a hot tip.

Isabel Guillermo had disappeared two months before her sixteenth birthday. And it was Alice's fault. Before that, Isabel had been placed into the foster care system. Also Alice's fault. Because Alice had had a bad day at work, Isabel's parents were dead. Again, Alice's fault.

A sweet and innocent teen's world had shattered because a criminal got one over on Alice. Her mistake had cost Sal and Patsy Guillermo their lives. Alice should've been more aware.

She shook off the reverie, focusing on the cowboy instead. Not only had he already located the canister, but he was standing perfectly still, studying her.

Alice pulled out her cell, grateful the downpour should provide enough of a curtain between them to mask her true emotions, and covered it with her free hand to shield it from the rain.

"We need to find another gas station," was all she managed to say. Thinking about Isabel's case, about the past few weeks, had her miss-

ing her boys. Her heart ached and she wanted
to be with them. But what kind of mother could
she ever be to them if she didn't find Isabel?

"ANYONE EXPECTING YOU at home?" Alice asked
the cowboy as he took his seat in the Jeep after
hiking for what felt like half the night to get
gas. She needed to know if she'd just put a
family in danger and that's the reason she told
herself she asked. His ride wasn't tricked out
for mudding so she figured it was his com-
mute vehicle.

"No."

Why did that one word make her heart flut-
ter?

Ignoring it, Alice thought about her next
move. Going back to get him had been impul-
sive and dangerous. She couldn't afford to take
unnecessary risks or rack up collateral damage. The cowboy would have to go with her to
her motel room. She hoped that he remained
cooperative so she could talk sense into him.

"Where to?" He turned the key in the ignition and the engine came to life.

"Take Highway 287 out of town," she said,
rubbing her temples.

"Mind if I stop for food first? There won't be
anything once we leave town and it's not like
you can order pizza from The Bluff Motel."

"How did you know where we were going?" She snapped her head to the left to get a good look at him.

"Not a lot of options around here."

Okay. Fine. He had her on that point.

"There a drive-thru nearby?" She needed something to eat and she could always hide in the backseat so no one saw her. Perez had eyes everywhere and she didn't want to risk anyone seeing the two of them together. No one should be looking for her, Perez or otherwise, at least not officially. Her SO had been texting for her return to work and to make sure she wasn't interfering with a federal investigation. She hadn't exactly broken any laws unless she counted unauthorized tampering with the National Crime Information Center—NCIC—database. As far as technicalities went, she wasn't exactly hacking into the system. She was just doing a little side research project.

Her stomach rumbled from hunger and her side ached. She needed to re-dress her stab wound, a gift from the last crime ring she'd infiltrated.

"We can zip through the line in a few minutes," he said, pulling into a burger stand parking lot.

"Okay." Eat. Rest. Talk the cowboy into witness protection. How hard could it be to convince someone to give up the only life they knew because of a perceived threat from a stranger?

"And then you'll come clean with why you're tracking one of the most dangerous criminal organizations in the country," the cowboy said with law enforcement authority.

Chapter Three

The motel room was basic but comfortable.
There were two full-size beds with a nightstand
in between, a small table with two chairs near
a picture window, and a dresser with an old-
fashioned TV. Joshua would bet money there
was a bible in the top drawer. The floral pattern in this room was bluebonnets, a nod to
the state flower, and they were on the curtain
and both bedspreads. The floor was tiled in a
neutral shade.

One of the bedspreads was rumpled and the
other bed was being used as a makeshift office.
Papers were spread out across the comforter
and there was a laptop along with a couple of
cell phones and a small technological device
that Joshua figured was for surveillance.

"Let's talk about your options," Alice said
after she'd finished the last bite of her burger
and drained her Coke. She wadded up the

wrapper and tossed it in the trash. They'd toweled off and she'd changed into dry clothes.

Joshua couldn't remember the last time he'd seen someone wolf down food so fast, and that was saying a lot given that he had five brothers.

"Or you could tell me what's really going on. Why you're on the run from the police," he countered, motioning toward the second bed, not ready to tip his own hand.

"I'm not—"

He put a hand up to stop her. "If you don't want to tell me why you're in this mess we'll bunk down for the night and I'll leave you alone in the morning. I have no interest in playing games."

The woman needed rest and the only reason he stuck around was because he figured she'd be crazy enough to follow him if he left her alone. Or so he lied to himself. There was more to it than that. He wasn't ready to acknowledge whatever "it" was because she mostly frustrated him.

She slipped off her shoes, settled against the headboard on the second bed and pinched her nose like she was trying to stem a headache. "I'm trying to find a young girl. It's my fault she's missing and, therefore, my responsibility to get her back."

Joshua turned his chair around to face her

and clasped his hands, resting his elbows on his knees.

"She disappeared six weeks ago and I've been searching for her ever since. With each passing day, her odds crash..." There was so much anguish in her voice that Joshua had to fight the urge to cross the room and pull her into his arms to comfort her. She'd probably poke him in the eyes if he did, he thought dryly, remembering how unwelcomed his attempts to make her feel better had been so far. She'd been clear on where she stood when it came to accepting help or being pitied. She'd taken a zero-tolerance stance.

"How old is she?"

Alice's eyes were closed now and distress was written all over her features. "Almost sixteen."

He couldn't even go there mentally...a place where one of his family members had disappeared. Two of his grown brothers had had brushes with death in recent months and that was enough to keep Joshua on full alert. They were adults capable of handling themselves. But a sixteen-year-old?

He flexed his fingers to keep his hands from fisting.

"I'm sorry," he said and meant it. Her admission explained a lot about why she'd be staying in an out-of-town motel, alone. "What happened?"

"She was around one day and then not the next." She opened her eyes and fixed her gaze on the wall directly in front of her. "You asked about me being on the job before. I used to be until this happened."

"You left to investigate this girl's disappearance?" he asked, thinking there were at least a half dozen scenarios where he would've done exactly the same thing.

She nodded.

"Why not do both?"

"We weren't getting anywhere on the investigation and my boss wanted my full attention on the job. I agreed, but on my own time I had to do everything I could to find her. The longer she was gone...well, let's just stay statistics weren't—*aren't* on her side. After three weeks of red tape and netting zero following procedure, I figured I could get a lot further my own way."

As a cop she'd have to follow procedure to a T when all she really wanted to do was find the girl and bring her home. She wasn't interested in prosecution and laws would get in the way.

"Did you quit the force?"

"Took an extended leave," she said. "But I have no idea if I'll have a job when I return.

The chief threatened me and told me not to interfere with an ongoing investigation."

"Bet you've covered a lot more distance than they have," Joshua said. A flicker crossed her features. Regret? Anxiety?

What was she holding back?

"I wouldn't know," she said, some of the tension leaving her shoulders. She bit back a yawn. "This guy I've been tracking is the real deal. He is going to come looking for you. It's not a matter of if, but when."

"He won't find me tonight," Joshua said. "He's probably still looking for the cute blond teenage girl who got away."

She laughed but her amusement disappeared too quickly. She zeroed in on him. "I'm serious. This guy is nothing to joke about. He's ruthless and no one has lived after catching him in action."

Joshua balked. "And you were trying to get him to take you so you could investigate this girl's disappearance?"

"Yes."

"That makes you either stupid or brave. I can't decide which." He admired her dedication. He also noted that it would take a whole lot of guilt to make a cop walk away from her job. "How many other organizations have you done this with?"

"Several."

"And that led you to Perez's group?"

She fixed her gaze on the ceiling. "He's my last hope of finding her and I tracked down a lead that says he's the one who took her."

"I'm guessing you saved him for last on purpose based on how dangerous he is." Joshua wasn't worried about being exposed to Perez. He wouldn't be sticking around in Bluff for long anyway. He'd been searching for the right time to tell his family that he had no plans to live out his life on the cattle ranch. Granted, he loved the land but he'd applied for a job in the FBI and had every intention of picking up his life where he'd left off once things were settled. A cranky little voice in the back of his mind asked, *Then why haven't you told anyone yet?*

The truth? He resented everyone's assumption that he'd drop everything and change his life. His older brothers might be fine with doing that, hell, they'd all spread out and made their own millions with successful businesses. They'd proven their worth as men. But Joshua was just getting going on his future. To have that stripped away just as it was getting good wasn't in the plans. As much as he loved his brothers, they wouldn't understand. His only regret—and it kept him awake at night—had been that he hadn't stepped up and told his father before he was gone.

Joshua had known on some level that his father wouldn't have liked his plan so he kept on living a lie, thinking that the right time to bring up the subject would magically present itself. The worst part was that the old man would never have expressed his disapproval. He was a good father. There was no way he'd make Joshua feel obligated. But Joshua had seen the look of excitement in his father's eyes last year when he'd told the boys about the plan to have them work the land he loved so much. He'd built a small empire for his sons from nothing. Rejecting his father's offer would make Joshua feel a lot like he was rejecting the man, his legacy.

Selfish as it might have been, Joshua hadn't wanted to see disappointment in his father's eyes. Now it was too late and he felt trapped.

"I thought I was alone with Perez and his men in that location. Never saw you coming," Alice admitted.

"How'd you know he'd be there?" he asked, redirecting his thoughts to something he could fix.

"I'd tracked him to the area based on a meeting he'd set up to talk to someone about a new transportation route and so I used an informant to plant a tip. I knew that if he could get me on Perez's radar that I'd have a good chance of becoming his target. My informant had already told me that Perez had a buyer for a sixteen-year-old blonde, so he set me up."

She'd fit the clean-cut American teenager to a T. Even now with her blue-striped pajama pants and white tank, she looked years younger. Her hair was drying and the rubber band looked barely able to contain her waves.

"And then you came along and…" She didn't say that he'd ruined it but he could tell based on her expression that's exactly what she was thinking.

"If I interrupted your plan to be kidnapped by one of the most dangerous men in the country, then I'm glad I came along when I did," Joshua said. He pointed to her right side below her armpit where blood flowered. "How bad is that?"

She glanced down and panic flitted across her face as she hopped up. "Oh."

"Don't move. You'll only make it worse." He glanced around the small room looking for some kind of emergency kit. "You have first aid supplies?"

"Not much. I meant to pick some up."

"Hold on." He ran out to the Jeep and retrieved his, shivering in the cold. The temperature must've dropped fifteen degrees in the last hour alone. On the ranch, he never knew when he'd need first aid so he'd gotten in the habit of keeping supplies on hand wherever he went.

The thunder had eased and the rain was coming down in a steady beat. He planned to head out at first light as soon as he knew she'd be okay.

Joshua returned to the room a few minutes later and found Alice as he'd left her. Head against the headboard with her eyes shut. Since her hand was closed around her Glock, he didn't want to startle her.

He moved closer so that he could disarm her if need be. He didn't take her skills lightly. She was good with a weapon but he was better. Couple that with the fact that exhaustion was slowing her reaction time and he had the edge he needed.

Her eyes snapped open the second the bed dipped under his weight.

"It's me," he said, his hand covering hers on the weapon as she brought it up. Physical contact sent a different kind of heat through him. A sexual attraction wasn't appropriate or wanted, especially under the circumstances.

She apologized and then shook her head.

"How long has it been since you've had a good night's sleep?" he asked. There were other more pressing questions he needed to ask, but he reminded himself not to get too personal with someone he would never see again after tonight. Because he had every intention of helping her and then getting back to the ranch to deal with his own problems.

"A while, I guess."

"What else do you know about Perez?" he asked to distract her as he lifted her shirt enough to see where the blood came from. He was worried about Alice. He peeled back the bloody bandage to reveal a two-inch gash three inches below her armpit.

"Most of these criminal rings take girls from places where huge crowds are gathered, like the Super Bowl. Not Perez. He searches for just the right one, looks for a certain kind and mostly prefers all-American types. He seems to have a particular affinity for blondes although Isabel—" she flashed her eyes at him as he cleaned the blood off the cut and then she continued "—that's her name, is a brunette. I can see why he'd take her, though, because she's a beautiful girl."

There was probably no way he could convince Alice to follow him to the ranch until he could dig deeper into the situation and things settled down. Her eyes were pure blue steel and determination and she'd left behind a job she loved to track down this girl. This was the closest she'd been to getting answers and he highly doubted he could convince her to slow down.

"Innocent girls and blondes fetch a higher price. His target age range is twelve to sixteen years old." She winced.

He apologized as he finished cleaning her wound, warning her that the next part might hurt more. "I'd be happy to take you to the ER."

Her head was already shaking before he could finish his sentence.

"Those are practically babies," Joshua ground out, thinking about what she said about the girls. Anger bit through his normally easygoing nature.

She nodded. "He likes to target places where there won't be a lot of extra security or cameras. Remote spots in small towns like this."

Joshua blotted her wound with fresh antibiotic ointment on a clean piece of gauze.

"Then, he sells them to various jerks or uses them to farm babies for high-profit adoptions," she said.

Didn't this conversation just spike Joshua's blood pressure in two seconds flat? No matter how many years he spent on the job he'd never get used to people who hurt children. He shook his head as he placed a new bandage over her cut.

"I learned that several of his girls have been used for the sole purpose of being impregnated and then held captive through multiple pregnancies," she continued.

Joshua knew all about those sickening operations. He'd get more information out of Alice if she believed he was a civilian. He pretended to be hearing this for the first time even though he didn't feel right deceiving her. "Do I want to know what Perez does once he...*uses* the girls?"

"Dumps the bodies once he's made enough from the babies and the girls start to become liabilities," she said with an involuntary shudder. "And that's just one of the things they could be doing with her. Perez has been known to sell them to a high bidder, which is why he likes a specific look. He knows the market and what his customers like. He gets a sense for their taste and then snatches a few girls to give a 'client' options."

Joshua had learned even more about illegal adoption rings when his oldest brother Dallas got involved with a woman whose baby was almost abducted before Halloween. Thankfully, Kate and baby Jackson were doing fine and Joshua figured a wedding announcement would be coming soon since Dallas and Kate had fallen in love during the process.

"I can't imagine the kind of monster it would take to do something like this to children," Joshua said, and then apologized as soon as he realized that Isabel was most likely in the hands of someone like that. By now, she could be pregnant, abused or dead. And that explained the worry lines etched in Alice's forehead. Being on the job, she would know firsthand what a deviant like Perez would do. And Joshua hated seeing her go through something like this when she should be home with Isabel, doing normal stuff girls do this time of year like holiday shopping.

"No need to be sorry," she said. "Believe me, it won't help Isabel."

"How do you know she didn't run away? Maybe she needed a change of scenery and she's somewhere safe in another city," he offered.

"We're close and I stay in touch with her foster parents and caseworker. She's a good girl and she loves my twins."

Joshua hadn't thought about the fact that Alice could be married with kids. She'd mentioned her boys earlier but he thought that was part of the lie she was making up about a relationship with Perez. He glanced at her ring finger and stifled the relief that came when he didn't see a band. But then she wouldn't wear one while on a case like this. "You're married?"

"No," she said.

He didn't want to admit the relief he felt with her answer. "You have twins?"

"Yeah. Why? You got something against twins?" Her eyebrow spiked.

"Nope. Not me." Joshua couldn't help but laugh given that he was a twin. His brother was the oldest by two minutes.

"It's not funny. I love them with all my heart but those two can be holy terrors."

"I'm sure they are." He smiled wryly thinking of all the misadventures he and Ryder had had. He was pretty certain his mother would've used that same term to describe the two of them.

"You have kids?" she asked.

"Nope."

"Then you have no idea what twins are like," she said so matter-of-factly that he laughed again. "What's so funny?"

"It's nothing." He wondered if his mother would have had the same exacerbation in her voice when describing him and his brother. The fact that she'd had six boys, the last of which were twins, made him certain she would.

THE COWBOY PUSHED off the bed. He'd done a nice job of dressing her wound.

"Mind if I grab a shower?" he asked.

"Not at all. I'll clean off the other bed for you," she said but he waved her off.

"I can manage. I'd rather you get some sleep." His jacket was already draped over the back of the second dining chair. He tugged his T-shirt up and over his head and then fanned it out to dry on the dresser.

Alice shouldn't let herself notice the ripples of muscles cascading down his back. He obviously spent some serious time at the gym. Then again, he'd mentioned something about a ranch. Working outside would give a man a body like his.

Tiredness pervaded every one of Alice's bones. There was no amount of caffeine that could keep her eyes open for much longer but she was so used to fighting sleep that she tossed and turned instead of giving in.

The fact that the cowboy was in the next room cleaning up shouldn't edge into her thoughts. Or that his body looked made of steel. It had to be the fact that she was overwrought with hormones combined with severe lack of sleep that had her thinking about the water rolling down the ripples in his chest that gave way to a solid six-pack stomach. She'd felt just how strong and masculine he was when her body had been pressed against his at the gas station. A place deep inside stirred, a need she'd felt too many times recently. She wished he could wrap those steel arms around her and make her feel safe.

How tired was she that her mind could wander to such a place given the circumstances? She forced her thoughts to the case and a sense of despair washed over her. It had been weeks since she'd seen her boys and that was probably the reason tears threatened so heavily this time. Or maybe it was the fact that the last lead to find Isabel had disappeared in front of her eyes. Perez wouldn't be looking for Alice, but if he ever saw her again her cover would be immediately blown. He'd been her last hope to find Isabel. She fingered the pendant on the necklace around her neck, half a heart. The other half belonged to Isabel. When put together they read Best Friends. Isabel had scrimped and saved to purchase the necklaces over the summer. Tears threatened as Alice thought about the gift she'd been planning to give Isabel.

Alice had planned to tell Isabel about her plans to file for adoption. She wanted to be more than a big sister to Isabel. She wanted to be family.

A dark sadness blanketed her like a thick fog rolling in. The clock was ticking, time was running out and Alice didn't know how much longer she could abandon her boys to chase down clues. Christmas was in three weeks and they deserved to have their mother home with them, too.

Alice hadn't been completely honest with the cowboy earlier. She'd kept to herself the fact that she'd been forced to step down from the case because she'd gotten too close to an existing investigation with the FBI. Tears spilled and a sob released as she thought about her options.

Alice hated her weakness, but she could no longer hold back the onslaught of emotions bearing down on her, suffocating her.

Chapter Four

Joshua hoped he'd get back to the motel before Alice woke. He'd slipped out to pick up breakfast supplies. Outside the local coffee shop, Dark Roast, he called his twin brother. Ryder picked up on the second ring.

"What's going on at the ranch today?" Joshua asked.

"Where are you?" Even though the sun wasn't up Ryder sounded wide awake, typical hours for a rancher. Joshua had always been more of a night owl. In fact, he'd done little more than doze off for a few minutes here and there in the past few hours. His seniority at the Denver PD had given him the right to choose his shift. Unlike his peers who worked the day shift, he'd picked evenings. Even though he'd been home for weeks, his internal clock hadn't made the adjustment.

"I'm in town at the coffee shop." It wasn't a lie.

"Don't tell me you have a hot date this early?" Ryder joked.

"Nothing like that. Just needed to make a run into town."

"How'd it go last night with the Nelson widow?" Ryder asked. He must've picked up on Joshua's tone and figured she was to blame.

"As well as can be expected when she opened the front door in a silk bathrobe." Joshua hadn't been thrilled.

Ryder laughed and that didn't help Joshua's mood.

"How'd you manage to get out of that one without hurting her feelings?" His brother must've known the widow would pull something. She always did.

"I pretended not to notice."

Ryder roared with laughter. "And she let you get away with that?"

"No, she let her robe fall open at one point," Joshua said, still not enthused. "I almost told her to go put on a turtleneck."

"That would have sent her into the other room crying," Ryder said defensively. "She's a little out there, lonely, but she's harmless."

"I didn't actually say that even though someone should. If you wanted diplomatic you should've sent Tyler." Joshua didn't hide his irritation. Their older brother was known for his ability to navigate sticky situations, evaluate all sides and come up with a solution everyone could live with. No doubt he would've handled the Nelson widow with ease.

"You don't have to bite my head off, man. I'm just here to shovel cow patties in the barn," Ryder shot back. "Besides, you're the one who drew the short straw at the family meeting last week."

That didn't cover the half of it. Joshua didn't mean to be terse with his brother. The two had always been close. Keeping his secret about applying to the FBI was eating at his conscience, especially as he moved through the rounds. Then there was the woman sleeping in the motel room twenty minutes away. "I haven't had my morning coffee yet. I don't mean to be a jerk."

"You're fine. Besides, the Nelson widow can have that effect on people," he teased, lightening the mood. "What's she donating this year?"

"A bronze statue called *Horse and Rider*. It's actually nice," Joshua said, thinking that an expensive piece of art like that needed to be out of the back of his Jeep before someone figured it was there and helped themselves to it.

"Sounds heavy," Ryder joked. "And classy."

"Should help with our fund-raising goal this year at the silent auction." He had no idea what that ultimate number was but he was sure a few of his brothers did, and rightfully so. They seemed like naturals when it came to stepping in for their parents.

"We ever going to talk about what's really been bugging you, because I know it's not the Nelson widow?" Leave it to Ryder to come right out with something on his mind. Then again, his twin would be the first to pick up on his underlying mood.

"It's just not the same without them at the ranch," Joshua said quietly, referring to their parents and that was 100 percent the truth. It was hard to think about being home without them there. And yet, that wasn't what was really bothering him. He hoped his brother would buy the excuse or give him a pass without digging further.

"I miss them, too." Ryder's tone said he was giving Joshua a pass. This conversation wasn't finished but would be saved for a later time.

"How's everything going this morning?" Joshua asked, ready to change the subject.

"Fine. Dallas and Tyler are out checking fences. Austin and Tyler are in the office today. Austin said something about being up to his neck in financials and Tyler is negotiating next year's supplier contracts. Are you coming in today? Uncle Ezra called last night and requested a family meeting," Ryder said.

"What's that about?" Joshua asked, distracted. He didn't feel good about leaving Alice alone. He checked his watch, 5:40. It'd been less than twelve hours since their first encounter with The Ghost. Perez could be anywhere. Based on his reputation he was most likely searching for Joshua, not Alice. Joshua still didn't like it. He scanned the parking lot aware that he had to watch his back a little more carefully until this whole situation blew over.

"I'm guessing he's fighting with Aunt Bea again and wants us on his side," Ryder said.

"Maybe he has another 'opportunity' for the family to invest in," Joshua quipped.

"Yea, like his others have been so successful." Ryder laughed.

Joshua tucked his free hand inside the front pocket of his jeans, staving off the morning chill. "What time's the meeting?"

"Said he'll come around suppertime. Think you can make it or do you need me to cover and then fill you in later?" Ryder asked.

"I'll do my best to be there. Can I text you later when I know for sure?" Joshua had missed three of the last four family meetings and he was starting to feel guilty. No matter what else he decided he would always need to be involved in the family business on some level. As for his life, he needed to set his priorities and work from there.

"Of course. I better get back to it. These cows don't clean up after themselves," Ryder said.

Joshua resisted making a snappy comeback as he ended the call. His next was to his friend, Sheriff Tommy Johnson.

"We got trouble in town," Joshua said after exchanging greetings.

"What happened?" Tommy asked, sounding half asleep.

"Did I wake you?" His friend was normally up and running by now.

"Not really. I've been working a case and didn't get much sleep last night. What's going on?" Tommy didn't say it but Joshua knew that his friend was staying up late working on his parents' case. He'd been poring over the guest list at the art auction the night before their deaths.

"Marco Perez was sighted last night at the gas station off Highway 287 near Harlan and he may be coming to Bluff next," Joshua said.

"What makes you think he'll come here?" Tommy asked.

"Me."

"Okay, back up and tell me everything." Tommy sounded wide awake now as ruffling noises came through the line.

Joshua relayed the details from last night up to the point of Alice taking him to her motel room. Even though it felt like he was betraying her, Tommy needed to know about any threats to the area. Joshua couldn't have innocent people being caught in the crossfire if Perez was on a hunting mission—the prey he was after might be Joshua. "Can you check out Alice Green? She's tracking these guys and she's a cop out of Tucson."

"Green. Got it," Tommy said. "I'll run her through the system."

"Would you mind keeping this quiet instead? Do you know anyone out west you could contact and ask unofficially?" Joshua didn't want to alert her boss to her whereabouts.

"I can't think of anyone offhand but I'll ask my deputies and see what we can come up with," Tommy replied after a thoughtful few seconds of silence.

"I'll owe you one." Joshua figured that line pretty much covered his morning, and his life ever since he'd clocked out the last time with Denver PD and returned to the ranch. He loved the land, there was no question about that, but living the life of a rancher was for his father, his brothers, not him. So, his twin had been doing nothing but covering for him. And Joshua couldn't keep up the charade much longer.

A SUDDEN NOISE woke Alice with a start. Heart thumping, she shot up and fumbled around for her Glock. The room was cast in darkness. Her heart raced at the sound of the door closing and the snick of the lock.

"It's just me," the familiar voice, the cowboy, said as a reading light clicked on. "And I brought coffee."

Alice sank onto the bed, trying to shake the feeling of heavy limbs that came with suddenly waking in the middle of a deep sleep. "Coffee sounds like heaven right now."

"How do you take yours?" he asked.

"Black works for me."

He handed over a cup and the warmth was amazing against her cold fingers.

"Okay if I turn on another light?" he asked.

"Sure." She took a sip, enjoying the dark roast taste and the burn in her throat.

"Mind if I join you?" He motioned toward the foot of the bed.

"Not at all." It was nice to have company for a change. She'd basically spent the past three weeks alone aside from being kidnapped, stabbed and burned. In all fairness, the burn was an accident. She missed her boys, home, her job. Even though she couldn't tell the cowboy everything about herself, she didn't have to pretend to be a sixteen-year-old with him.

Alice glanced around the room. "Someone around here is into bluebonnets."

"It's the state flower."

"I know that." She took another sip. "I'm not an idiot."

"Never said you were." He arched his eyebrow.

Okay, she was probably being too defensive. She needed to tone down her attitude. "Thanks for the coffee, by the way. I appreciate it."

He nodded and half smiled. "How's your side?"

"No fresh blood. That's a good sign." She lifted her shirt enough to get a good look at the bandage.

"We'll need to clean up the wound this morning to make sure infection doesn't set in."

"Hold on a second, cowboy. *We* don't need to do anything. I've got this." Her defenses were set to high gear again.

He shot her a disgusted look that she didn't want to overanalyze.

"Of course you do," he said.

Well at least he took a hint. Or so she thought.

Until he got up, moved to the bathroom and then returned with the first aid kit he'd stashed there last night.

"I'm not the most agreeable person before coffee and I think we've gotten off on the wrong foot this morning," she started but he interrupted her. He was trying to help and, although that grated on her, she also realized how nice it was to have a friend.

"Letting me clean and bandage your wound doesn't make you dependent on me, or weak." He spoke slowly as though he didn't want to leave any question about his intentions. There was also a sharp edge to his voice.

"I never said it did," she protested but he was already by her side, kneeling down. And if it wasn't for those intense green eyes of his she'd stop him right there.

"Then lift up your shirt and quit being a baby about it," he dared.

Alice did and then took a sip of coffee, realizing for the first time in weeks just how tired she was. Her still-foggy brain wasn't helping with her disposition. The caffeine was starting to make headway toward clearing it. As it was, she'd been running on power bars and adrenaline, and even though she'd slept like a champ last night she knew it barely scratched the surface of what she really needed. Careful not to hurt her already aching side, she tried to stretch the kinks out of her arms and legs.

"I need to come up with a new plan," she said on a heavy sigh, not sure why she was confiding in the cowboy.

"Since I have no confidence in your plan-making abilities, I'm willing to offer my services," he said with a smile.

"Great. Thanks for the confidence," she said and then laughed. The cowboy had a point. And a great smile. "I guess I can see where I might look a little crazy from someone else's point of view."

"Desperate or determined are probably better words. I just don't want you to get yourself killed in the process," he said. Maybe it was too early in the morning and Alice's brain hadn't fully engaged but the deep timbre of his voice sent sensual shivers down her back. "Why don't you tell me what you've done and where you've been so far? We can go from there."

Alice took another sip of coffee and then leaned her head against the headboard. She took in a deep breath and closed her eyes. "Okay. Let's see. Isabel went missing six weeks ago."

"And we've already determined that she's not a disappear-with-a-band type," he said with another endearing half smile.

"She's more of a Taylor Swift person," Alice said, wishing she could return the smile. Just talking about Isabel made her heart ache.

"When did you realize she was gone?" He said the last word quietly and his reverence was duly noted and appreciated.

"We were supposed to meet at Lucky Joe's Café right after school. She didn't show." Alice took another sip and opened her eyes.

"Is that when you realized something was wrong?"

"No. Not right away. I called her first and her phone went straight into voice mail. I thought maybe she got tied up with a teacher. She'd been stressing over her upcoming exams and didn't feel prepared. The whole semester had been stressful. I thought maybe she was biting off more than she could chew. She's a motivated student and she signed up for AP World History, Pre-AP Chemistry, Pre-AP English, and Pre-AP Algebra 2. Even though she speaks fluent Spanish, she signed up for AP French."

"Sounds like an intense load," he said. "I think I took one AP class before graduating."

"Times have changed. Kids push themselves harder these days. Isabel wanted to get a college scholarship and she had no athletic ability."

"So, she had to push herself that hard?" His dark brow arched.

"She thought she did. Her parents didn't leave her any money and she didn't have any other family in the US. The rest of her family is poor and live in Mexico. Conditions are worse there. She wanted to stay in the States and make a better life."

"Why don't you sound convinced?"

"Part of it was true. I do think she wanted to make a better life for herself but I also believe she was pushing herself so hard because she wanted to keep busy. Not deal with the fact that her parents were gone or that her foster parents didn't care. She and her parents were close-knit and I could see how much she missed them." An emotion passed behind the cowboy's eyes that she couldn't quite put her finger on. He didn't say anything, so she kept going. "She'd been spending a lot of extra time at school, going to tutoring early in the mornings and staying late so I figured she forgot about our plans."

"And you're sure that's all she was doing?" the cowboy asked.

Alice shot him a look.

"Whoa. Don't get mad at me. I have to ask and you know it." He put his hands up in the surrender position, still gripping his coffee with his right. "Don't mind me. I'm just a rancher."

Alice noted that he seemed to be pretty darn

good at asking questions for someone claiming to work on a ranch. A simple life sounded damn amazing to her at this point. Was there a place she could get away with Isabel and the twins? Away from the world and all the stressors it contained? Or did a place like that even exist? Alice was anxious and that was the only reason she was thinking about escaping. The truth was that she loved everything about her job except for the guilt that came with making a critical mistake. When she had a bad day, someone could die.

The thought sat bitterly on her chest.

"Isabel didn't have a lot of friends. Her school counselor said she'd always been a shy, bookish girl. She never got into trouble."

"Did she have *any* friends?"

"No one close. She liked school and turned all her homework in on time."

"You mentioned that she was feeling overwhelmed with her studies," he said.

"Well, yeah, wouldn't you? She was pushing herself too hard and I told her that I thought she should lighten her load," Alice said.

"How did she respond?"

"She agreed with me. But the school wouldn't let her change out of her Pre-AP classes until the end of the semester. She was worried about her GPA dropping in the meantime, so she started going to all available tutoring sessions," Alice defended.

"Which is the reason you didn't think too much about her blowing off a meeting with you?" he asked.

"I should've realized she was in trouble or that something had happened right then. She was dependable. I should've known that she would've shown if she'd been able to." Alice couldn't hold back the tears threatening any more than she could stop the heavy feeling pressing down on her chest. "I should've sounded the alarm right then and maybe we would've found her before she was taken out of town."

"Hold on there a second," the cowboy said. "Had she ever missed a meeting with you before?"

"Well, yes. Once or twice at midterms," she supplied, trying to tamp down her guilt before it overwhelmed her and tears flooded.

"So, this time was no different than before. Experience had taught you that when Isabel got stressed she could get distracted like any normal human being, let alone a fifteen-year-old." His words stemmed the flow of tears burning the backs of her eyes.

"I guess you're right. I just keep replaying that day over and over again in my mind trying to figure out what I could've done to stop all this from happening in the first place," she admitted, unsure why she was dumping the truth on a complete stranger. Maybe it was easier to confess her sins to someone she didn't know and would never see again once she left Bluff, Texas.

"Unless you have some kind of crystal ball that's not possible." His tone was matter-of-fact.

She took a minute to let those words sink in.

The cowboy spoke first. "When did you realize she was missing?"

"Not until the next morning when her foster parents called, Kelly and Bill Hardings. Kelly assumed that she'd gone home with me to spend the night. When the school called the next morning to say she didn't show up, they called to find out what was going on."

"Sounds like they cared about her," he said and she could tell he was reaching for something positive out of the situation.

"I think they were more worried about them looking bad to the state. They'd already talked to her caseworker about having her removed from their house and replaced with someone younger," she said, frustration rising.

"Why would they do that? She sounds like the perfect foster kid. Studied hard. Got good grades."

"She's also fifteen, which pretty much means

moody and self-absorbed. Don't get me wrong, she's a great kid. But teenagers aren't exactly the easiest people to deal with. Plus, Isabel still hadn't gotten over missing her parents so she didn't really open up to them like they'd hoped."

"Why take her on in the first place? They had to know what they were getting into."

"I'm not sure they did. They were new. After reading her file I think they thought she'd be a good way to get their feet wet with foster care. And then when she didn't bond with them right away they got discouraged." Alice knew that scene a little too well.

"I don't understand that thinking. I mean, either you want to help or you don't. These are human beings we're talking about not pieces of furniture." She appreciated the outrage in his tone because she felt the same way.

"The caseworker said the couple is asking for someone quite a bit younger next time." Alice bit back her anger. "Isabel is a good kid and she doesn't deserve any of this."

The look of compassion in the cowboy's eyes was like comforting arms around her. Alice needed to change the subject and get back on track. She didn't deserve to feel at ease until Isabel was home. "Fast forward to that next morning after I got the call from the Hardings.

After contacting Isabel's caseworker and confirming she hadn't heard from her, I pleaded with my boss to issue an AMBER Alert. The Hardings filed the paperwork, so he did. At that point, we had to assume it was a stranger abduction since she had no relatives near."

"And you already knew something was very wrong by that point," he said.

She nodded before taking another sip of coffee.

"What did you do next?" he asked.

"I started investigating right away. Went to the school and talked to the last person who saw her, her AP World History teacher. He didn't notice anything unusual that day. Neither did her other teachers. I already said she didn't have a lot of friends but the few she had didn't notice anything strange."

"How far was Lucky Joe's from her school and how was she planning to get there?" he asked.

"It's across town. She had to take two city buses, which I didn't like. I volunteered to pick her up from school but she insisted on taking the bus. Said it was good practice for when she left for college and that she needed to learn how to get around on her own. She was almost sixteen and most people were already driving. I think she was worried about me being in the car instead of spending time with the boys. I work the evening shift and that means I don't get home until the boys are already in bed most days."

"I already know you spoke to the bus drivers. What did they say?" he asked.

"Isabel never made it on to the second one. There's a half hour wait in between buses. Again, I didn't like it but she said it gave her a chance to get ahead on her homework so she could focus on me and the boys during our visit." Those words were getting harder and harder to choke out. Isabel's connection to Alice also made it harder for her to bond with the foster family. Alice would've stepped aside if she'd believed that was best for Isabel but she never did fully trust that Kelly and Bill had Isabel's best interests at heart. So, she'd interceded and bonded with Isabel, which most likely messed up her foster situation. Alice had messed that up for Isabel, too.

Chapter Five

"I already know you canvassed the area, so I'm guessing no one claims to have seen her," Joshua said. Alice bore the weight of the world on her shoulders and he found himself wishing there was something he could do to ease her burden.

She cocked her head to the side and stared at him for a long moment before answering. Joshua needed to be more careful or his cover would be blown and she'd stop talking.

"Either that or no one wanted to admit to seeing something, which doesn't surprise me since I've narrowed down the possibilities to The Ghost. He's powerful in the small area of town we live in, in the southeast of Tucson. The locals wouldn't dare go up against him. They fear him too much. There are other criminal groups there, too. The people in small towns off Interstate 10 know to look the other way if they want to keep their own families safe. Everyone is aware of human trafficking and prays that it never happens to one of their own," she said.

"Sounds like a great place for criminals to thrive."

Alice nodded. "There are three main groups with strong footing there—the Santos, the Giselles and Perez."

"You've already ruled out the first two." He motioned toward the stab wound on her side, trying to keep her focused on something besides putting the pieces together that he was in law enforcement. Her exhaustion worked in his favor.

Alice may be bone-tired but she was still smart. *And beautiful*, an annoying little voice in his head added.

"That's right. I'm down to Perez," she said. Her forehead crinkled when she was frustrated.

"You already mentioned that your informant set you up."

"That's right," she said. "In fact, I need to touch base with him this morning. I meant to do that last night."

"Sounds like he was taking his life in his hands in order to help," Joshua said. The pieces of what Alice had been through were starting to fit together and he was beginning to understand the depth of her guilt.

"It was that or go to jail for the rest of his life," she said quickly. "I gave him an out if he'd help me."

"What about Isabel's cell phone records?" he asked.

Alice motioned toward the other bed. "Whoever got to her must've taken away her phone and destroyed it. I couldn't trace her using the GPS I'd downloaded. You can look at the log if you want. It's over in that stack of papers. Basically, she didn't make any calls all day while she was in school. Me and her foster parents were the last people calling her cell."

"At least they cared enough about her to try to track her down," he offered, trying to ease some of her remorse.

"Really? Check the records. They phoned all of once at nine o'clock at night, which was the time she was supposed to be home. They went to sleep and got up the next morning not concerned enough about her to call me to make sure she made it in the first place," she said.

"What about since then? It's been six weeks, surely they've had some reaction to all this," he said. Now that her cover was blown with Perez she needed to come up with another plan that didn't include being abducted by the most dangerous criminal in America. And if she had to go after Perez, it would be best to gather evidence and present it to a law enforcement agency who could then go in for the bust. He had a strong feeling she'd never go for this idea.

"I haven't spoken to them since the first week." Alice absently toyed with the lid to her now-empty coffee cup.

"And how did they act then?" he asked.

"Shocked and grieved at first. Maybe a little relieved, too. Like a problem had been solved."

"Have you ruled them out as suspects?" he asked. He didn't like to think someone who had been trusted with a child could do anything horrible, but his experience in Denver had shown him otherwise. "They would've known the route she was taking that day."

"True. Everyone was a suspect in my mind at first. I had my boss interview them because a) I was biased and b) it was a conflict of interest given our relationship. They met up with friends for dinner and a movie. I checked into their financials in case they benefitted financially from her disappearance and there was nothing."

"You got access to their financial records that quickly?" It was too fast for her to have gone through proper channels.

She shrugged, kept on talking, "None of

their actions so far have indicated they were involved. There'd be a trail. They had no financial difficulty other than the usual things like still paying off student loan debt. His job is stable and she works part-time at a bank. Neither has bought a new car and they haven't taken an expensive vacation. I've looked at every possible angle and they came up clean."

"What about Isabel's caseworker?" he asked.

"Michelle Grant? She's actually decent. I'd spoken to her about Isabel's file a few times and she listened to my concerns. She was keeping an eye on Kelly and Bill, and their relationship with Isabel based on my concerns."

"When was the last time you spoke with her?"

"Three, maybe four weeks ago. Why?"

Hearing Alice's thoughts on the investigation and the people involved helped Joshua put a picture together. Based on what she'd told him so far, she was a solid investigator. "I can tell that you're depriving yourself of sleep and you've been doing all this on your own. Thought it might help to talk through your leads so far."

"I've dotted all the *i*'s and crossed all the *t*'s. I'm convinced this has to be Perez's group."

"And what if it's not? Plus, you can't exactly

go waltzing back in there now. If he sees you he'll figure you out right away."

Suddenly her cup of empty coffee became the most interesting thing in the room based on how intensely she studied it. Was he getting through?

"If we go back and retrace your steps we have a better chance at finding her," he said, trying to drive home his point.

Alice sat motionless for a few minutes that stretched out before nodding her head. "You're right."

She struggled to bite down a yawn.

A wave of relief rippled through him. Joshua wasn't sure how he'd come to care so much in such a short time about a stranger—maybe he could relate to her determination to do the right thing and her sense of guilt—but he wanted to help Alice. No one should carry a burden like hers alone.

"That pretty much highlights what I've done. What's our next step, cowboy?" she asked, sounding resigned and maybe a little hopeful. "It's good to get fresh eyes on the investigation."

"I can take a few days off from the ranch." He didn't even want to touch the thought of how easily that statement rolled off his tongue.

"It won't take long to travel to Arizona. We can leave tonight."

"Good idea." She nodded her head. "Arizona is the last place Perez would be expecting to see either of us."

"If what you said is true he'll stick around here a few days trying to find me. It would be smart to change our appearances."

"Right again." She smiled and maybe it was the spark of hope in her eyes that stirred something dormant in his chest.

Joshua didn't want to think about that. He was just glad that something moved in there. Since taking leave from the force, he could admit to feeling empty inside. He should have an interview or a rejection from the FBI coming soon. In the case of a job offer, he'd have to find a way to tell his brothers that he had no plans to return to the ranch. How in the hell was he supposed to do that? They were counting on him to do his part. As for his father's disappointment…he couldn't even go there right now.

If the FBI offered, he had every intention of accepting on the spot even though he knew it'd be a couple of months before he could officially start. The agency would need to complete a background check and he'd have to pass the physical—no problem there because he kept up his training. Other than his brothers, there wasn't anyone special in his life that he'd need to talk over the decision with. And why did that fact suddenly make his life feel like it was missing something? Or, more appropriately, *someone*. Being alone had never bothered him before. What had suddenly changed? *Hold on there, O'Brien.* Joshua wasn't touching that one, either. He refocused his thoughts on the investigation. He wanted to talk to the Hardings himself and get a feel for them. Years of training and experience had honed his instincts into a fine-tuned machine and he'd get an accurate feel for them after one good conversation. He trusted Alice's instincts, too. He also couldn't ignore her bias toward the couple.

Also, he wanted to talk to Alice's supervising officer to see if he had any new information on the case. If this case was important to Alice, it would be important to everyone she knew at work. Cops operated that way, like more of a family than coworkers. Hopefully, Tommy could help with the connection since Joshua didn't know anyone in Tucson.

"You hungry?" he asked after poring over the intel she'd gathered. All of which led to the same conclusion—Perez. Her source had believed a teenager with Isabel's description had been a target. But then the guy was a two-time loser heroin addict going for a get-out-of-jail-free card. Alice was so hungry and desperate to find Isabel she would have been willing to take just about anyone's word at face value. Her judgment was blinded and that's why it's never a good idea for an officer to work on a case too close to his or her heart. It's the reason doing so was considered a conflict of interest. She'd want to see something so desperately that she could miss real clues. Of course, mentioning the possibility to her would most likely get him a boot out the door. In her defensive state, she wouldn't appreciate having her judgment questioned.

"Do you happen to have any food stashed in your Jeep outside?" She stretched again, winced and he could tell she was holding in just how much movement hurt.

"I can do better than that. I'll pick up breakfast burritos. Bacon or sausage?" he asked.

"Bacon," she said with a slight smile, easing off the bed. "I'll clean up while you're gone."

Joshua took the last drink of coffee before tossing the cup. He'd offer to help her walk to the bathroom but figured that would just get him another look and he didn't want to do anything to jeopardize the progress he'd made so far in gaining her trust. Instead, he walked out to his Jeep, shivering in the cold morning air.

The breakfast run was going to take a few minutes more than Joshua had anticipated because the line in the drive-thru extended to the street. He'd forgotten all about the fact that it was a weekend. He also thought about the expensive piece of art in the back. He'd need to swing by the ranch before heading out of town or have one of his brothers meet him somewhere to make the exchange. It would be about a fifteen-hour drive to Tucson or they could cut the time dramatically if they flew. It'd be easy enough to arrange a car to be waiting at a private airport if they decided to fly and that would keep them off the highways where Perez and his men could be waiting, watching. The air might be their safest bet and especially since he could control how many people knew about the trip.

He'd paid and moved to the second window of the Burrito Barn when his cell buzzed. It was Tommy, so he used Bluetooth to answer as he took the food bags from the smiling redheaded attendant and thanked her.

"I have news on the name you gave me," Tommy started right in.

"Good or bad?" Joshua didn't like his friend's tone as he rolled up his window and pulled out of the drive-thru lane.

"She's in trouble with her employer in Tucson. How well do you know this person?" Tommy asked.

"What kind of trouble?" Joshua dodged the question.

"I've been advised to bring her in for her own good or have her stay put so someone can pick her up."

"She's wanted for questioning?" Sure, she'd dodged a few rules going out on her own to investigate this case. Joshua understood that her SO would probably be angry if she wasn't following the law to the letter. That was most likely the reason she'd gone off the rails in the first place. She needed answers, not red tape, and especially since a little girl's life hung in the balance—a girl Alice felt responsible for.

"It's worse than that. She disappeared in the midst of a Professional Standards Department investigation."

"What did the Professional Standards Department want with her?" he asked, but he already suspected that he knew the answer to that question based on his earlier discussion with her.

"To talk to her about charges of tampering with evidence in a federal investigation," Tommy said.

"Whoa. Hold on there. A federal investigation?" Joshua asked, not liking the sound of those words. If his involvement with Alice came to light, his application, his future could be ruined.

"Yes. And her SO said that if she didn't get herself back to the station soon there'll be nothing he can do to protect her. He's already covered for her as much as he can without jeopardizing his own job."

Damn.

"We're heading to Tucson tonight." Joshua trusted Tommy with his life but he didn't want to give his friend any specific details that might put him in an awkward position. Sharing the information that they'd be on a plane tonight would constitute prior knowledge and Tommy couldn't lie in court about it. "I'll convince her to go in and clear this whole ordeal up with Professional Standards."

"Good. I have everyone on alert for Perez. I'm guessing these two are connected in some way."

"It's best to hang up now," Joshua said, again thinking about how his friend might have to testify in court and that it would be best if Tommy didn't know everything.

"You sure about that?" Tommy asked.

"Keep eyes out for Perez. I'll give you a call after I get Alice to her station house."

Tommy agreed to the last part, so Joshua

didn't argue. He was pulling into the parking lot of The Bluff Motel and his stomach was reacting to the smell of the burritos. There'd be no time to stop off at the ranch. Joshua owed a call to one of his brothers to give them the statue. He decided to text his twin brother, Ryder, instead. He picked a location near town and set the time. Ryder confirmed a few seconds later.

At least the rain had let up from last night. The sun was out but a cold front had moved in overnight just as promised and the temperature was hovering a bit above freezing.

Joshua wondered if Alice had brought any warm clothes with her. At least his had dried out. The door to the motel room would be locked, so he knocked and waited.

Was she still in the bathroom? Surely she wasn't showering longer than forty-five minutes. She might've dozed off again while she waited for him. She looked more than exhausted earlier and he figured that was half the reason she hadn't pegged him for a cop yet. He had no plans to tell her about his background even though it felt like a deception, and those were mounting. Keeping things from the people he was closest to was beginning to be a habit, he thought as he knocked louder this time.

Still no answer and that fact spiked his blood pressure. What if Perez had found her?

Don't do that, O'Brien. Don't make assumptions.

Joshua made a quick dash toward the motel's front office.

A bell chimed as he opened the door and the attendant looked up from the newspaper spread out on the counter in front of him. The older man smiled to acknowledge Joshua. He was leaned forward over the paper and must've been sitting on a stool. He had on a mint-green button-down shirt that looked a size too big.

"Something I can help you with this morning?" he asked.

"I'm visiting a friend in room 115 and she's not answering the door." He heard how that sounded the minute it came out of his mouth. He held up the food bag. "She called and asked if I'd bring over something to eat. Said she wasn't feeling well last night. Stomach bug or something but now she was starving."

"I have the key right here. I'd be happy to check on her." The idea someone might've messed up the room etched a frown line across his forehead.

"I'd appreciate it."

"Hold on. You want to take a seat?" the man asked.

Joshua introduced himself.

"I'm Sherman." The old man took the hand being offered.

"Any chance I can follow you, Sherman? She didn't sound good this morning when I talked to her and I want to see for myself that she's okay," Joshua pressed.

"As long as you stay outside the room," Sherman said. "I reckon' it'll be all right if you take a peek."

Joshua didn't want to touch how poorly that spoke to security at The Bluff Motel as he followed Sherman out the front door. He waited as Sherman posted the out of the office sign before locking the door.

"Let's see here." Sherman held the key up as he shuffled his feet, moving forward at a hair faster than a snail's pace. "You said room 115."

"Yes." Joshua shouldn't be impatient with the older man but his danger instincts kicked up, telling him something was wrong.

Sherman paused in front of the door and it was all Joshua could do not to take the key and open the door himself.

"Here we go," Sherman said, opening the door and stepping aside. His nose wrinkled like he expected to be hit with the stench of vomit.

Joshua stepped inside the doorjamb ahead of Sherman. There was nothing. No smell. No mess. No Alice. Worst of all, there was no sign she'd ever been there, either. The secondary bed had been cleaned off and there wasn't so much as a scrap of paper lying around.

"Where could she have gone?" Joshua asked out loud, forgetting that he had company.

"Maybe she got to feeling better and took off."

"Would you mind checking the bathroom? Just to make sure it's clear?" Joshua asked, stepping aside to allow Sherman access.

"Sure thing," Sherman said but the tone of his voice said he didn't expect to find anything.

Joshua turned and leaned against one side of the doorjamb while he waited for the old man to shuffle across the room.

"No sign of her in here, either. Looks like she left in a hurry, though," he said.

A thought dawned on Joshua. He hadn't questioned the fact that Alice had asked if he had a vehicle last night. It hadn't occurred to him that she would have one of her own. And by taking his, the question of what she drove never even came up. He had no idea what to look for on the road.

Basically, she could've driven right past him on his way back to the motel and he never would've realized.

ALICE CROUCHED DOWN low in the field next to the trailer another half hour from The Bluff Motel off Highway 287 going west. Her informant had texted her last night about Perez's whereabouts and she hadn't checked her phone until the cowboy had gone for breakfast.

Even if Dale hadn't sent that text she'd been prepared to walk away from Joshua. His investigation skills were a little too highly honed for him to be a simple rancher and he didn't seem to be inclined to share his background with her. He'd gone with the rancher cover and she'd pretended to believe it, all the while plotting her escape. She'd tricked him. Mission accomplished. So, why did she feel like such a jerk? It wasn't like she really knew the guy.

Alice tried to shrug off the feeling. The truth was that she was an honest person. No one hated lies more than Alice. Had she been doing her fair share lately? Yes, she thought with a sharp sigh. Her back was against the wall when it came to Isabel and she was bending rules she knew better than to break, none of which made her feel comfortable. Then there was the internal investigation she had ducked out of back at the precinct. No matter how pure her reasons were, Alice knew there'd be a price to pay for her actions.

She mentally shook off her reverie and refocused on the 1990s single-wide Palm Harbor trailer in front of her. Her body was already soaked from lying in the still-wet grass and she was thinking about that warm cup of coffee she'd had earlier in an attempt to stave off the shivers rocking her. Being from Arizona, she didn't exactly own a winter coat and the light jacket she had on did little to brace her against the cold, unforgiving earth.

Isabel had to be Alice's priority right now. Nothing else mattered, she tried to lie to herself. She missed her boys. The thought of being away from her babies for their first Christmas ripped up her insides and yet how could she enjoy the season while Isabel's future was so uncertain?

The boys were too young to know what day it was. If she missed Christmas with them, she'd put up a tree anyway and make her own day. If her worst fears came true she wouldn't have a job to go back to anyway. Meaning she'd have a lot of free time while she figured out her next move.

A part of her she didn't want to acknowledge missed the cowboy, too. And that was as productive as packing herself in ice to stay warm.

Holidays or not, handsome cowboy or not, Alice had to stay focused.

She glanced at her watch. She'd already been staking out the place four hours and not one person had come or gone.

A station wagon drove up the gravel lane fifty yards away from her by the time she looked up. There wasn't another trailer for a couple of miles. Alice watched as the white station wagon pulled in front of the trailer. There were two guys in the front who exited the vehicle simultaneously.

This was her first real break since blowing the setup last night. If she could get a good look, she could ID the guys, maybe even snap a picture. Her hands were stiff from cold. She flexed her fingers a few times to warm them up.

Alice pulled binoculars out of her backpack, trying to erase thoughts of Joshua O'Brien out of her mind...which would be a lot easier if she didn't see him, unconscious, being hauled out of the backseat of the station wagon and up the pair of wooden steps into the trailer.

Chapter Six

Alice needed a plan, like, right now. Otherwise all her efforts to save the cowboy last night would be for nothing. Okay, what would she do if she was Perez or one of his men?

First she'd interview the cowboy to find out what he knew and/or if he'd told others about the operation to determine if there was additional threat. Perez would also want to know why he'd shown up the other night to help her. There was no way Joshua O'Brien was going to give him or his men anything, which would leave Perez with no choice but to try to torture the information out of him.

Again, she couldn't see a scenario in which the cowboy would talk. So Perez or one of his men would kill Joshua. She couldn't stand by and let that happen.

So, if Perez wasn't there, his men would need a direct order to dispose of the cowboy.

There was no way they'd act without permission. They'd need to check in with their boss first, which introduced a variable since Perez might not be available right away. That could buy Alice precious time. Even a few minutes could mean the difference between life and death for Joshua.

One thing was certain, the cowboy wouldn't talk and they would kill him.

There was another important variable she had to consider. She had no idea how many men she was up against. The station wagon was the only vehicle parked out front but that didn't mean there weren't others inside or on their way. There was no time for recon and she couldn't take the risk of getting close to the trailer and being caught anyway.

This seemed like a good time to curse the fact that she'd been waiting for it to get dark outside before she tried to get closer to the trailer, which was hours away on a bitterly cold day. That fact also fell into the category of Things She Could Not Fix. So, she moved on.

Other factors that she didn't like included the idea that she had no clue how many or what kind of weapons Perez's men had inside those walls. For all she knew, this could be where they kept an arsenal. And then there was the fact that she wasn't familiar with the layout of the trailer, although she could formulate a decent guess based on the year it was built and her experience having carried out busts in several other trailers over the course of her law enforcement career.

The front door, which she currently had eyes on, would lead straight into the living room, based on its position to the right of center. On the immediate right would be a hallway with a couple of secondary bedrooms and a bath. To the left would be the kitchen and the master bedroom with an en suite. The back door would most likely be off the kitchen. She closed her eyes and envisioned the layout, recalling all the details of the last trailer she was in, walking through it in her mind.

Joshua could be anywhere inside. Going in blitzkrieg style without knowing how many men she was up against could end up getting them both killed. She needed to create a diversion and get them outside so she could count them.

Alice willed her hands to stop shaking, a combination of cold and adrenaline, as she fumbled with the zipper on her backpack. What could she use? Papers? Maps? GPS device? She mentally shook her head. None of those were useful as of now.

An idea sparked as she pulled out matches

and then quickly died as she examined them. They were soaking wet and therefore no use to her. However, could she figure out a way to light a fire somewhere like the cowboy had in the field?

Her mind zipped through the possibilities of setting a blaze to the field, the trailer—catch the trailer on fire and Joshua might burn with it—or the station wagon. Hold on. That last thought might work. Best she could tell it was the only vehicle around and that would mean their only form of transportation. Surely that would draw the men out since they'd need to put out the fire or risk it catching the trailer, as close as it was parked. In fact, if the car exploded, the windows of the trailer might blow out and cause injury to someone inside.

She palmed her cell. She'd downloaded an app that had scrambled her location in the event her co-workers or boss, or the feds, decided to take matters into their own hands and look for her. It would come in handy now because she would need to call 9-1-1. On the off chance the fire wasn't enough to clear the place, sirens would make criminals scatter faster than deer catching the scent of a hunter.

The fact that the men would have no transportation would make it easier for the police to catch them.

Okay, so, burn the station wagon and call 9-1-1 was the plan, adding arson to her growing list of felonies.

Now, what could she use to start a fire since her matches were soaked?

The soggy packet in the palm of her hand mocked her. Since they would do no good she tossed them inside her backpack.

Maybe there was something closer to the trailer. Alice shouldered her backpack, stuffed her cell in her front pocket and then belly-crawled across the slick grass. She climbed under the wood slats in the fence and then circled the perimeter to check out the backyard, giving the trailer a wide berth and keeping with the tree line.

When she was within twenty yards of the place, the back door opened so hard it smacked against the wall. She suppressed a yelp and froze, praying she was camouflaged against the landscape.

A man hopped down the couple of stairs with a lit cigarette hanging out of the side of his mouth. She may have just found her fire source.

Alice scarcely breathed while waiting for the stocky guy in his early-to mid-twenties to finish his smoke. She was losing precious minutes and the feeling of being stuck there doing nothing while God only knew what was happening to Joshua was like heavy weights pressing on her shoulders. Her teeth chattered from the cold and being on the frigid, wet ground sent chills through her body.

The smoker finally took the last drag off his cigarette after what felt like an eternity and then flicked it onto the ground. He hopped up the couple of steps and disappeared into what she figured was the kitchen area.

As she neared the trailer, the silence was deafening. She tried not to think about what might be going on inside as she surveyed the area. In order to reach the butt—which she could only pray was still burning—she'd have to get within ten feet of the back door. A risky move.

While she was still out of earshot, Alice fished her cell from her front pocket and called 9-1-1. In barely a whisper, she reported a car fire, gave an address and then ended the call. That way, if she was caught while retrieving the cigarette butt law enforcement would arrive soon enough and that would give her and Joshua a fighting chance. The call was basically backup insurance. This being a rural location, she figured it would take at least fifteen minutes, maybe more, for a deputy to show. And that also meant she needed to kick her bottom into high gear because a deputy would be expecting a car fire.

Belly down, Alice crawled toward the spot where she estimated the smoker had flicked the butt. She should see smoke by now. Maybe she'd miscalculated. She double-checked her positioning against the back door.

Alice searched the ground. This should be near the spot but she saw nothing. A mild breeze was blowing and that could be the problem. She prayed the wind was the culprit because she was running short on ideas, had waterlogged matches in her backpack and Joshua was in trouble.

Besides, there was no way on earth she could be at the trailer when the sheriff or one of his deputies arrived. Time was ticking and the cigarette butt was hiding.

There, she caught sight of a sliver of brown less than an inch long. That had to be it. She crawled closer, praying this would be the break she needed.

There was no fire. The wet earth must've put it out. Damn. Damn. Damn.

Desperation made her arms hard to lift as she rolled onto the ground on her side. A loud masculine grunt came from inside the trailer, kicking another wave of adrenaline coursing through her. *Joshua!* She pushed up onto all fours and scurried around the other side of the trailer determined to find something she could use to ignite a flame.

Rocks battered her knees and cut her palms as she navigated onto the makeshift driveway. She didn't dare raise to her full height, even though the trailer was positioned on cinder blocks making the windows high. But she couldn't stay on all fours, either. She forced herself into a crouching position, keenly aware that she'd aggravated the cut on her side, causing it to bleed again. She could deal with the fallout from that later. For now, all she could focus on was getting Joshua out of that trailer and to safety. It was the least she could do after the way he'd put his life on the line to save her. In fact, it was her fault he was in this position in the first place.

There was nothing obvious out front that she could use to light a fire, so hopes of finding something inside the station wagon were her last resort. The door was unlocked and that was the first break she'd gotten all day. The second came when she found a half-empty pack of cigarettes on the dashboard. The smoker. He would have multiple sources of fire. Since bad news came in threes, she prayed the same was true for the opposite. She smoothed her hand across the seats and deep into the joint where the bottom met the backrest. She scanned the floorboards and ran her hands under the seats. Surely, there were matches or a lighter in there somewhere. The station wagon was too new to have a built-in lighter.

There was a Google Maps printout folded and tucked between the driver's seat and the console. She grabbed it with her left hand, continuing to search with her right.

Her fingers stopped on a small plastic piece. Could it be? She closed her fingers around it and pulled it out...a lighter.

Alice dropped her right shoulder, causing the backpack to tumble to the ground. She fumbled with the zipper, wincing as pain ripped through her side, and tucked the page into the side pocket. She pulled out a few of her own papers and twisted several together before locating the release latch for the gas container.

Somehow, she was supposed to set this baby ablaze without injuring herself and then get around the back of the trailer to the rear door unseen. She planned to slip inside, find Joshua and free him before the bad guys came back in—provided they all left in the first place—and then get the heck out of Dodge before anyone from law enforcement arrived.

There were more holes in her plan than a piece of aged cheese and her good luck had already run out. And just to make things a little more interesting, Alice heard the faint roar of sirens in the distance.

Alice zipped her backpack and shouldered it. She moved toward the rear driver's side of the vehicle and to the gas line. The door was already open so she removed the cap. She lit one end of the paper, said a quick prayer and then stuffed the dry end of the paper into the gas line. Fumes blew out a burst of fire, catching her right forearm before she could pull her hand back fast enough. She immediately dropped to her knees to get out of the way.

The station wagon was about to go *boom*.

Her fight, freeze or flight response kicked in from there as she ignored the pain piercing her side. She scampered to the side of the trailer, located the biggest rock she could find and then tossed it toward the vehicle. The alarm system engaged, piercing the air with shrill beeps.

One and then two men burst out of the front door, the ones from earlier. Alice cleared the back of the trailer at the same instant a loud *boom* sounded. She instinctively dropped to her knees and located her Glock, palming it.

The sheriff or some other law enforcement official was nearing and Joshua was still trapped in there with those jerks. Talk about a plan unraveling. The worst part was that she might've just made it worse for him. Part of her feared she'd hear a gunshot. And then there was the fresh burn that wrapped around her forearm. It was already red and looked angry. She figured shock was the only thing keeping the pain away. For now, at least.

Then she heard voices out front as the sounds of the fire ravaged the rest of the vehicle. She raced to the couple of steps at the back door away from the voices, anxious to find Joshua and get out of there.

The back door was unlocked. Thankfully. So she took a risk, opened it, and bolted inside letting her Glock lead the way.

Alice stopped in the kitchen, quickly scanning the area. The living room was next. Something was wrong. Why was there so much smoke inside the trailer? She coughed, taking in a lungful of thick gray air. Her eyes started to burn. She needed to find the cowboy and get out of there.

The kitchen was clear. She moved to the living room and beyond the couch that had been blocking her view. A man was rolled up on his side, unconscious. "Joshua."

Sirens grew louder as Alice cleared the hallway, the bedrooms, and then returned to the cowboy. She couldn't risk putting her gun away and helping him until she knew it would be safe. Running to an injured person without clearing a crime scene would be a rookie mistake. She tucked her Glock inside her backpack and dragged the cowboy across the carpet and then the laminate flooring to the back door. Smoke filled the room and she had no idea if there'd be another blast. All she knew for certain was that they had to go.

Her lungs felt like they would seize as she gasped for fresh air. He was a solid mass and dragging him was taking all her strength. It was all she could do to get him out the door and to the tree line, hoping they'd be able to disappear there long enough to catch her breath and get a second wind.

As it was, her head was dizzy, her vision blurred and pain ricocheted through her body. She wasn't sure what hurt more, her side, her burned arm or her lungs. Two steps inside the tall grass and safety of the trees, Alice collapsed onto the ground next to the cowboy. She faintly registered that he looked different but then she'd never seen him unconscious before, either.

No matter how hard she tried to fight, exhaustion wrapped long-lean fingers around the edges of her consciousness. There was no way she'd be able to keep it at bay much longer.

Footsteps registered, not from the direction of the trailer but the trees behind it. That couldn't be a good sign, she thought, as she gave in to the darkness.

THERE WERE TWO bodies slumped over in the woods twenty feet ahead of Joshua. He immediately called Tommy and briefed him. Even though this wasn't his jurisdiction, he could call in favors should Joshua get into trouble. As he closed the distance between him and the bodies, he made them out to be Alice and his twin brother, Ryder. Guilt was a hot brand searing his heart because this was his fault. He'd been on his way to meet Ryder at the Tastee Freez Old Fashioned Ice Cream stand and hand over the bronze statue when he'd witnessed the entire scene. Two men in their early-to mid-twenties driving a late-model white station wagon had pulled in next to Ryder, who'd parked in the back lot away from other cars. Ryder had been staring down at his phone, no doubt texting Joshua to see how close he was to their meet-up point. The red light at the intersection had detained him.

The first man had exited his vehicle and stretched. Ryder had glanced up but didn't think twice about it and neither had Joshua at first. The second, the one closest to Ryder, had exited next but his brother had already dismissed any threat, his eyes glued to the device in his hand.

Joshua hadn't thought much of that either, figuring his years of police work had him overly paranoid when he started committing their descriptions to memory. What could he say? Old habits might die hard for others but not for Joshua. He was law enforcement through and through.

Even so, the entire situation had seemed non-threatening until guy number two, the short and stocky one, pulled a gun and pointed it directly at Ryder's forehead and forced him inside the station wagon. It had taken every ounce of self-discipline for Joshua not to stomp the gas pedal and roar into the parking lot. His training had kicked in, overriding his adrenaline rush, so he'd forced himself to breathe slower and take measured action instead of blindly reacting to the situation playing out in front of him. One wrong step and they could both end up kidnapped or killed.

Because Joshua was late, his brother had been abducted. Now, he lay wounded and unconscious in the woods in rural Texas. Joshua had tracked those jerks who'd taken his brother, making sure he wasn't detected and then he'd been making his way through the thick mesquites for half an hour trying to find the damn trailer from the back side of the property. If only he'd arrived ten minutes sooner and not ended up lost in the damn trees.

The explosion followed by flames had jump-started his adrenaline again. His heart had stopped for a few seconds until he coughed to force it into action and started running toward the smoke.

Guilt seared him. He'd deal with the fallout from his emotions later. Right now, he had two unconscious—at least he hoped like hell they were unconscious because that would mean they were still breathing—and injured people to get to safety. He dropped to his knees next to the bodies, watching their chests, praying for movement. Ryder was facedown in the wet weeds and Alice was curled on her side, her skin pale. Her lips were blue. Both she and Ryder were still breathing, and that was the first time Joshua released the breath he'd been holding since initially identifying them.

There was a flurry of activity at the trailer and law enforcement would descend on these woods at any moment. Getting the two of them out of there undetected became his number one priority.

Retracing his steps would be easier now that he'd gotten his bearings. His Jeep was fifteen minutes away by foot. He needed to assess their injuries and figure out how he could get them out of there.

Carefully, he examined their injuries. Ryder had a serious gash in his forehead that needed to be dealt with and between the pair of them Alice looked to be in worse shape. The cut on her side was bleeding, her shirt soaked red. She'd picked up second degree burns on her right forearm that would need medical treatment. He rolled up a shirt from her backpack and put pressure on her cut to stem the bleeding. He had a few supplies in the Jeep. No. He didn't. He'd taken them into her motel room last night. Speaking of which, given what he knew about her circumstances, turning her in or taking her to the hospital would ensure her losing her job in law enforcement. He instantly regretted calling Tommy.

There were more pressing things than jobs right now, like, getting these two the hell out of these woods. In a few minutes, the trailer, woods and beyond would be crawling with deputies and Joshua didn't want to lie to law enforcement. Besides, he had two unconscious people to tend to and both needed medical attention.

He pulled water from Alice's pack and poured a little over Ryder's forehead to get a good look at the cut. It was a flesh wound, so that was a relief, despite the amount of blood dripping down his face. Forehead cuts were known for their bleeding. Ryder's eyes blinked open. And that was the second relief.

"Thank... God, you're awake," Joshua said, praying his brother would keep his eyes open.

Ryder looked around, seemed to be trying to get his bearings. "What happened?"

"There's a pretty good cut on your forehead," Joshua said, scanning his brother for any other injuries. From the looks of it, he'd taken a few shots to the face and there could be trauma. "Do you know who I am?"

"The less good-looking of a set of twins," Ryder quipped, his hand coming up to his forehead. "What happened? My head hurts like hell."

"You don't want to touch that," Joshua warned, thankful his brother wasn't showing signs of a concussion. He'd keep an eye on him, though. "The cut isn't too deep but it's bloody."

"Figures," Ryder said with a smirk. "I'm all show and no substance."

And that was the second bit of good news. If Ryder's sense of humor was intact he was going to be fine.

"Who jumped me?" he asked, making a move to sit up, wincing with pain.

"Go slow there, buddy," Joshua said, grateful

his brother would be okay. Seeing him lying there on the ground hadn't done great things to Joshua's blood pressure.

Ryder glanced toward the trailer. "I can rest later. We gotta get the hell out of here."

"Think you can walk?" Joshua asked.

"I plan to." His brother's resolve was one of the many things Joshua appreciated about his twin. "What's the deal with her?"

"I'm guessing she's the one who pulled you out of that trailer," Joshua said.

"Like that?" Ryder's voice showed his shock as he motioned toward her injuries.

Joshua nodded. "Let's get her to safety and treat both of your injuries then figure out what happened."

"That's the best plan I've heard all day," Ryder agreed, accepting help up from Joshua to stand.

Next, Joshua picked up Alice. Even though she was fierce and he knew how much she insisted on taking care of herself she seemed small and soft cradled in his arms. Being a cop, he understood her thinking but he also needed to teach her that accepting help from him wasn't a sign of weakness. "My Jeep isn't far. Lean on me and we'll get there faster."

"I can walk on my own. Your hands are full

with her," Ryder said, wincing and sucking in a burst of air when he put weight on his right leg. His brother didn't know the half of it.

Chapter Seven

"What happened?" Alice gasped as she bolted upright. Of course, her mind would snap to the last thing she remembered.

"Hold on there. You're okay, you're safe," Joshua tried to soothe her. He could see confusion in her wide blue eyes and she was disoriented, which he'd expected. It was the middle of the night, pitch-black outside. His eyes had long ago adjusted to the dark while he stayed by Alice's side, not wanting her to wake up scared or alone after the ordeal she'd endured to save his brother. "Lie back down and try to relax."

She reached up to tug on her oxygen mask.

"Doc said you could take that off once you woke. You breathed in a lot of smoke and she mumbled something about oxygen levels and preferring to take you to the ER," he said as he moved to her side and then sat on the edge of the bed. He did his level best to calm her panic as he helped her adjust the oxygen mask so she could talk.

"Where am I?" she asked. "Wait a minute. You were hurt. I dragged you from a trailer in the woods. There was blood all over your face. Your forehead was covered in it."

"I'm fine," he said and a place deep in his heart stirred at seeing how concerned she was about him. "That was my twin brother you saved. His name is Ryder and we both owe you for what you did. You're at Dr. McConnell's house. She's a family friend, taking care of you at her home on a favor, and only agreed to treat you here because I gave my word you'd stick around until she said you were well enough to leave."

Confusion knitted her brow.

He'd given her a lot to digest at one time. He wished there was more he could do to take the fear out of her eyes.

"Hold on a second. You're a twin?" Her look of shock tugged at his heart. He hadn't exactly deceived her and yet the feeling was the same.

"Yes." He'd planned to tell her at some point but there hadn't exactly been a good time.

"Why didn't you tell me that before?"

"We didn't get around to talking about it," he said, which netted a cross look from Alice. "I didn't tell you before because there's a girl out there who needs our help." That part was true enough. "And as long as we're confessing our sins…why did you disappear on me?"

Alice shifted her position, looking uncomfortable. "What branch of law enforcement did you work in?"

"You didn't answer my question," he said, moving to adjust the pillows so she could sit more comfortably. "Is that better?"

She nodded and didn't meet his gaze. "I left the motel because I had a tip from my informant."

"It couldn't wait until I got back?" he asked. "In case you're still wondering, I'm on your side."

"How could I know that for sure? I kept you around because I thought you might end up getting hurt if I left you alone. The reason you got yourself into trouble was because you were trying to help me. Once I realized you were in law enforcement I knew you could take care of yourself, so I took off to follow a lead."

"Your informant told you about the trailer?" Joshua asked. He'd been wondering how she knew about that location.

"Yes. I thought maybe they were holding girls there since it was out in the sticks."

"And you hoped that either Isabel was there

or one of the girls would know where she'd been taken?" It was more statement than question.

She nodded.

"Want me to turn on the light?" he asked.

"Yes. Please. What time is it?"

"Two twenty-five in the morning," he said, flipping the switch on the soft light next to the bed. The warm glow brightened the room and he could see her anguish clearly on her face. "What can I get for you? Water? Food?"

"Nothing, no, wait. Water," she said, examining the bandage covering her right forearm.

He made a move to get up but her hand stopped him and he did his level best to ignore the jolt of electricity spreading through him from the point of contact.

"Hold on. First of all, thank you for saving me. I owe you one," she said.

"Best as I can figure, we're even," he said with a half smile.

"Tell me what happened before you go. How'd I get this?" She motioned toward the extra-large white bandage covering her arm wrist to elbow.

"I'm not sure. I found you with these injuries, so I'm guessing this happened while you were trying to save my brother." He repositioned the pillows behind her so she could sit up more easily, thinking about the fact that she'd put herself in harm's way again trying to save the person she believed to be him.

"My cut was bleeding. Did you stop it?" She pushed the covers down to expose her side. "Wait. How'd I get into pajamas?"

"That was me and the doctor I told you about." He tried to push the images of the soft curve of her hip and the long lines of her legs out of his mind. He'd been a gentleman and looked away as soon as he could.

"She treated your cut and your burns, most of which are second-degree. We have a salve to put on twice a day and we have to keep the burns dressed, especially once they blister."

"And you arranged all this?" she asked suspiciously as she glanced around the room.

"You saved my brother. For that, I owed you." He was grateful to have Dr. McConnell as a friend. The woman was country to the core from wearing jeans and boots underneath her lab coat to the rustic Southwest feel of her home. The queen-size bed was positioned as the focal point of the room. The headboard and footboard were each made of a single large pine log with log side rails. A thick burgundy bedspread contrasted with the light-colored wood.

The walls were painted a light gray shade that reminded him of a chilly, winter sky—the kind that made him want to throw a few logs onto the fireplace and stay in, stay warm. "You lost a lot of blood. Doc groaned a little bit about me not taking you to the ER, but I asked her to treat you here instead." He could only imagine how weird it would be to wake up in a strange bed next to a man she barely knew after sustaining the kind of injuries she had. "I should wake the doc, so she can check on you while I get you that water."

Her fingers touched his forearm again. She pulled back when he stared like she'd just touched him with a branding iron.

"The other night at the motel was the first night I've really slept in a long time," she said.

Joshua didn't want to give away his real reaction to her, especially since his attraction was completely out of place under the circumstances.

"How's your brother?" she asked.

"I've had better days," Ryder said from his position in the doorway.

"How long have you been up?" Joshua asked, turning toward his brother's voice. He stood and then covered the distance between them in a few short strides to embrace his brother in a bear hug.

"Half an hour maybe," Ryder responded. He looked tons better than he had a few hours ago.

McConnell had insisted that he stay with her, too. Joshua had seconded her argument, preferring to keep watch on his brother while he healed.

"Take a seat." Joshua pointed toward the side chair. "You shouldn't be walking around yet."

"I made it out of the woods," Ryder quipped and they both chuckled at his bad pun.

"Even so, I'd feel better if you took a load off," Joshua said with a wry grin.

Ryder nodded, but stopped short of letting Joshua help him walk to the chair.

"This is my brother Ryder," Joshua said to Alice as she studied his brother's features.

After a thoughtful pause, she said, "No wonder I thought he was you. You two look almost identical."

"Yeah, but I'm the better-looking twin," Ryder teased.

"Still holding on to that dream?" Joshua shot back.

"I have a mirror. I know what I see. Then I look at you. Doesn't take a rocket scientist to figure it out."

"You also have a head injury," Joshua pointed out with a smirk.

"Shots fired. Looks like I'm taking aggressive action," Ryder kept the joke going, shooting a pleading look toward Alice, who smiled back.

Joshua loved all of his brothers but he and his twin had always had a special bond, the kind that made long explanations unnecessary. Which made keeping a secret from him feel even worse and especially one as big as he was holding on to.

The two used to joke that they knew what the other one was thinking without needing to say the words. Most of the time, Joshua enjoyed their special bond. But when it came to his career move and Alice, he'd rather keep his brother in the dark a little while longer.

Especially where it applied to Alice. He had yet to figure that one out for himself.

ALICE COULDN'T HELP but notice the ease with which Joshua and his brother spoke to each other, the obvious love they had for one other. They shared the kind of relationship she wanted and hoped for her own boys.

In her job, she saw the bad side of people. Families at odds. Husbands hurting their wives. Abuse. Being witness to too much of the dark side of humanity had tainted her view, if not extinguished all hope there was something better, something more to people and relationships.

There was still a spark in her that believed in people who did the right things for the sake of honesty. Men who loved their wives, families, and didn't hurt their children. Even if her personal experience had mirrored more of her professional experience.

"Do you have any siblings?" Ryder asked Alice.

The question caught her off guard.

"No. It was just me," Alice answered, hating the lonely edge to her voice when she said the words out loud. Now that she'd started down that slippery slope she figured she might as well go all in. "My dad disappeared before my first birthday and my mom was killed on her way to work a few years later."

The look of surprise and compassion on both men's faces brought stinging tears to the backs of her eyes as both offered apologies. This wasn't the sort of thing she ever talked about with people. In fact, she'd been holding it all inside so long. Looking at Joshua, seeing sympathy and not condemnation, gave her the strength to power on. "I'd started kindergarten by the time I had to be moved from my first foster family. They were religious zealots and believed in hitting first and asking questions later."

Joshua returned to his seat on the bed and

she could felt the mattress dip under his weight. The concern in his eyes turned darker, like clouds as a storm brewed. His eyes were how she could tell the difference between the brothers. Joshua's were so green, almost like clear emeralds, whereas his brother's were more hazel. Both of the men had black hair—Joshua's was darker and a little curlier—and she wondered if dark hair was an O'Brien trademark.

Joshua also had a freckle by his left ear. She told herself it was the cop in her needing to memorize every detail and not the woman.

"The second and fourth foster families weren't bad. Neither had bet on a long-term assignment when they'd taken me into their homes. They were emergency relief when a placement went wrong." She didn't want to think about the nonemergency families having spent the better part of her life trying to block those out. Her experiences varied from people who wanted money from the state and "free" help around the house to "fathers" who wanted easy prey. Alice had stabbed one with kitchen scissors; he lived. She simply ran away after fighting off the next one, figuring she'd fare better on her own. "By the time I was a teenager, I figured I'd do better on my own. Figured it might be easier than fighting off some of my male guardians. Got caught after two weeks, which turned out to be a good thing. I was placed with a retired sheriff and his wife. They were kind and I was able to bring up my grades enough in high school to get into a local college." She looked up at the brothers and realized she'd been a little too chatty. Her cheeks flamed. "Sorry. I don't usually tell my life story to strangers."

"Don't be," Joshua said quickly.

The room was suddenly too quiet and Alice could hear her own breathing. Had she shared too much? Looking at Joshua made her heart race and especially seeing the intense look on his face that said he could read between the lines of what she was saying.

"Are you feeling better?" Alice asked Ryder, trying to change the subject and calm her racing pulse.

Joshua covered her hand with his; that little bit of contact spread warmth through her.

Ryder smiled sympathetically before nodding. "I owe you for saving my hide. If you hadn't been *there*… I wouldn't be *here* right now."

"We both owe you," Joshua said and there was an emotion in his voice she couldn't quite put her finger on. Regret? But that didn't make sense, did it?

"I have a feeling both of you would've done the same thing for me," she countered. "One of you already has."

A gray-haired no-nonsense-looking middle-aged woman with rounded shoulders stepped into the room. Her hair was cut short, just above her ears and to the collar in back.

"What's my patient doing out of bed in the middle of the night?" she asked, staring at Ryder.

"I was getting a drink before going to the bathroom, ma'am," he said, the utmost respect in his voice as he grinned at his brother like he was about to be sent to the principal's office.

Joshua made a move to help his brother up, but Ryder wasn't having it. He waved off his twin as he grimaced. "I'm getting out of here in the morning and heading back to the ranch."

"We'll see about that," Dr. McConnell said.

"If you get the green light, I'll call to make arrangements for you to be transported safely." Joshua was all business when it came to his brother's life. "You'll need to lay low until we catch this son of a—"

"Not with a lady in the house," the doctor interrupted, clucking her tongue.

Alice suppressed a chuckle. Besides, it hurt to laugh.

"My apologies, ma'am. I didn't mean to

offend." Joshua tipped an imaginary hat toward Alice.

"Apology accepted." She winked, grateful for the lighter conversation.

Joshua moved from his spot presumably to give the doctor better access. He walked a step behind Ryder with his hands up, ready, in case his brother needed him but without Ryder even knowing he was doing it. Witnessing the two of them together stirred her heart in so many ways. Their parents had done something right in raising these men and she hoped to do half as well with her own boys despite the seeds of doubt that reminded her she had no idea what she was doing in the parenting department. She absently fingered the half-heart charm necklace resting on her chest as the doctor pulled a stethoscope from around her neck.

The exam didn't take more than a few minutes and the doctor gave her a stern warning about movement. "If you need to go to the bathroom, ask for help."

Alice glanced from Joshua to the doctor and must've blushed because the doctor quickly added, "He'll help you to the door and wait outside until you say it's okay if I'm not around."

McConnell reinforced her recommendations of hydration and bed rest before turning off the light.

"It's good that your brother is going to be okay," Alice said in the dark once the doc had gone. She was still thinking about the close bond between the two men.

"Thanks to you." There was that edge in his voice, like earlier. Then it dawned on her why. Joshua blamed himself.

"It's not your fault," she said.

"You don't want to go down that road," he said quietly. There was a warning in his tone but no real threat.

"Which one?" She wasn't ready to move on from the topic and maybe it was because she recognized guilt when she heard it, saw it. Leaving a teenager to ride the bus on her own and not immediately sounding an alarm when she didn't show was a good reason to be guilty. Looking too much like your twin was not.

"I know what you're trying to do here, but leave it alone," he said.

"It's not your fault, Joshua."

"I put him in harm's way. I may as well have tossed him to Perez and his men on a platter."

"You had no idea any of this would happen," she countered, not ready to let him take all the blame. "If you remember correctly you were just trying to save me and that's what got you into this mess in the first place. You were doing the right thing in helping what you thought was a teenager in trouble. That's how Perez spotted you. That's why his men are after you. And all that is because I tried to do undercover work that I wasn't authorized to do. If anyone's to blame, it's me."

"Not so easy. I make my own choices and I take responsibility for them. You didn't ask for my help and I think we both know you wouldn't have. I still have the bruise on my left arm from you being frustrated about that one. He's my brother. I didn't warn him about Perez. This is on me. Besides, you don't get to corner the market on all the guilt."

Was that true? Had she been making herself responsible for everyone around her? Always turning every situation that went sour into her fault? Yeah, the cowboy was probably right. Didn't change the fact that neither O'Brien would be on the run or hurt if it hadn't been for her carelessness.

"I should've known better. Perez was after me and I didn't connect the dots that my own twin brother might be in danger. How stupid does that make me?"

"From my point of view?" she asked but it was rhetorical. "You're always trying to put others first. That's the whole reason you inter-vened in the field. And you've been trying to keep me out of trouble ever since. If anyone's taking the blame for Ryder being jumped, it's me. I never should have taken off like that without telling you."

If he really believed what he was saying about himself what did he think of her? She'd messed up big time with Isabel. Did the cowboy blame Alice as much as she blamed herself?

The room went quiet and she could tell he was turning over what she'd said in his mind.

"You didn't say what happened to your mom," Joshua whispered after several silent beats had passed. "Is it okay to ask about her?"

"Yeah, sure. It happened a long time ago. Her body was found exactly two months after the day she disappeared. She'd been strangled and then dumped on the side of the highway. The case was never solved," Alice said with as much detachment as she could muster. The truth was that she would never stop wondering what had happened to her mother and how different her own life might have turned out if she hadn't been shuffled into the system. Would she be able to trust? Because not trusting anyone, ever, and always expecting the worst, was exhausting.

"That the reason you went into law enforcement? Needing answers in your mother's case?"

"Probably. At least part of it."

"The sheriff must've made a good impression," Joshua said after another thoughtful pause.

"I admired him for how much he cared about people, strangers." Her own father hadn't cared enough to stick around but there was no use sinking into that self-pity hole. Feeling sorry for herself didn't change her situation and only made her bitter.

"For what it's worth, I'm sorry about everything you've been through," Joshua said. She could tell that he meant every word and there was something about hearing it that eased her burden. "No one and especially not a kid should have had to endure any of it."

"It's not your fault, but I appreciate what you're sayin'." It was pitch-black in the room and she couldn't see a hand in front of her face if she wanted to and yet she felt comforted while talking to Joshua. What was it about darkness that made it seem safe to spill secrets? Or was it the cowboy's presence that made her feel that way?

"It wasn't yours, either," he said quietly.

She let that thought hang in the air, waiting for her eyes to adjust.

"I know that you don't want to lose momentum in the investigation, so I'm planning on going out tomorrow to recheck the site. I need to know what all you've gotten yourself into," he said matter-of-factly.

"Sharing won't be a problem for me. I won't hold anything back as soon as you tell me which branch of law enforcement you work for," she said.

Joshua sat there, silent, as her eyes were beginning to adjust to the dark. She could make out his basic form if not the details of his face. She wished she could see his expression so she'd know if he was about to lie.

"I'm on leave from my job as a cop in Denver, trying to decide my next move." His steady, even tone said he was telling the truth.

"Why would you leave the force for a cattle ranch?" she asked, quickly adding, "Not that cattle are bad. It just seems like a drastic change."

"My parents died and I inherited part of the family property. It was always assumed that I'd come back and take my rightful place with my brothers to help run things," he said.

She picked up on the way he'd said *assumed*, like he had no say in the decision. Joshua O'Brien didn't strike her as the kind of man who would roll over on something as important as the work he did. Before she could ask, he stood.

"I'm going to check on my brother. Do you

need anything while I'm up?" he asked, the topic clearly closed.

"No. Thanks. I'm fine."

He stopped at the doorway. "Are you really?"

"I will be when I get Isabel back."

MORNING CAME AND the smell of fresh-cooked eggs and bacon streamed through the hallway and into Alice's room. She eased to a sitting position, trying not to think about how much movement hurt. She needed to get back on track with the investigation but there was no way she could do anything in her present condition.

Joshua appeared in the doorway with a tray of what smelled like heaven on earth. "I thought you might be hungry."

"Starving." She figured it was a peace offering after the way things ended last night.

"Doc said that would be a good sign. She's doing rounds at the hospital this morning and said she'd drop by on her lunch hour to check on her favorite patient."

"Me?"

"I know she wasn't talking about my brother." He laughed as he set the tray on her lap.

"How is he, by the way?" she asked, taking the mug of coffee first.

"Sleeping. Better. He'll be fine. He didn't

sustain a serious enough blow to worry the doc. She wants him to stay until she gets here and then she figures she'll cut him loose." Joshua took his seat, clasped his hands together and rested his elbows on his knees.

That wasn't a good sign because his body language said he was closing up on her.

"What is it?" she asked.

"I have something to say and you're not going to like it."

She took another sip to clear her mind.

"I spoke to the sheriff this morning."

She started to protest but he cut her off.

"Before you get riled up, hear me out."

She picked up the fork and toyed with the eggs, staring intently at them.

"Here's the deal. You already know about my law enforcement background and that's why I know how important it is to follow protocol if you ever want your job back. I also know about the situation with Professional Standards—"

She tried to cut him off again with similar results.

"Maybe you don't want to work in law enforcement again, and that's fine. Either way, I want to give you the option."

"You have my attention." She dug into a chunk of scrambled egg and pushed it into her mouth. It was probably too late to save her job but it would be helpful in trying to raise the twins if she wasn't in jail for obstruction. The thought of doing something that could separate her from her boys, and especially with no father in the picture, threatened to eat away at what was left of her stomach lining.

"I know the feds are involved and you've ignored everyone's warnings to butt out of this case. Tommy is a friend of mine and he wants to speak to you as a witness," he said. "You don't have to worry. He isn't planning on arresting you or giving up your location to your SO."

Alice chewed the eggs.

"Before you tell me what a bad idea all this is I'd like to point out that you're in no condition to do any of this on your own," he added. "You need me at the very least and I need to bring in help to do this the right way and avoid anyone else getting hurt."

That much was true. She wouldn't argue there.

"You have strict instructions to rest and I've been told to apply salve to your burns and redress them twice a day," Joshua seemed to add that part to further his point of her needing to accept help.

"Is that why my burns don't hurt? Some miracle salve?" she asked, considering his proposition. She thought about lighting the station wagon on fire, the blaze…and then remembered the printout she'd taken from in between the driver's seat and console a few moments before she lit the paper and stuffed it in the gas line.

"Where's my backpack?" She frantically scanned the room. The piece of paper could mean nothing more than a family gathering or restaurant location but she'd seen cases blown wide open with less.

"It's in the kitchen." He didn't ask if she wanted him to get it. He seemed to sense the importance of it as he cleared the room and returned a few seconds later. "What am I looking for and where?"

"In the front compartment."

Joshua pulled out the Google map, shooting Alice a warning look. "No. We're not going to investigate this ourselves. You're going to finish your breakfast and I'm going to send for the sheriff."

"But—"

"Nothing. You're in no shape to confront these guys and they most likely assume I'm dead."

"They'll know you're alive when they read the news and learn there were no bodies in the trailer."

"Details about the incident are being suppressed," he said.

"Your sheriff has that much power?"

"Here locally, yes. But that's not why."

Alice knew what he was going to say before he said it.

"You already know the feds are involved because they told you if you didn't leave this alone they'd haul you to jail on obstruction charges," he said.

"So you already know," she said. "They'll do it anyway as soon as I surface. They have to know I've been involved."

"Not necessarily. Tommy's working on your behalf. Giving him this map will help prove that you're willing to step aside and let them do their jobs. You act otherwise and none of us will be able to help you or keep you out of jail."

"They would still be clueless if it weren't for me. I'm getting further than they are on my own and they'll mess everything up for me if I let them in," she countered, knowing full well they didn't care about her or Isabel. All they wanted was Perez.

"I understand where you're coming from and I have to think that they do, too, on some level." Joshua's tone had softened. "So, I'm not asking you to do this for them. I'm asking you to do it so you can be around this Christmas for your boys. They need you. Isabel needs you. And we have to do this the right way or you could lose everything."

The weight of those last four words sat heavy on her chest.

Everything the cowboy said made sense. She knew in her heart that he was looking out for her best interests and so was her SO. She could give it another chance with the sheriff's support. The feds couldn't be trusted. They'd been clear that they were willing to sacrifice Isabel for a bigger conviction. Granted, she wanted Perez or whoever had Isabel to go to jail for the rest of his life but Isabel would always come first. If Alice had the chance to swoop in and get Isabel away from Perez's operation she wouldn't think twice even if it meant jeopardizing the bigger case.

"Call your friend. I'll tell him everything I know about Perez's operation and what I've found out so far if he promises me to put Isabel first," she said.

"Deal. He'll do the right thing. You can trust him," Joshua seemed to read her worried thoughts.

Show her a cop with blind faith in people and she'd expose the real Santa Claus.

Chapter Eight

"Thanks for coming on such short notice," Joshua said to Tommy at the front door.

"I'm not sure how you convinced her to talk to me." Tommy glanced around the living room.

"We want the same things," Joshua responded. "Trust is going to be an issue for her."

"She's a cop, so I figured as much," Tommy said.

"It's more than that. Her dad abandoned her at a young age. Her mother was murdered. Then she was shuffled around the system." Her fierce determination to protect Isabel made even more sense to him now. Because of a mistake she felt that she'd condemned a young girl to the same fate as her own—a fate that hadn't been kind.

"I'm guessing that didn't work out too well for her," Tommy said.

"Not until a retired sheriff and his wife stepped up to the plate. She was in high school by then." Joshua also figured it was the only reason she'd agreed to speak to another sheriff instead of one of her own. He could also see the attraction in becoming an officer because cops were all about the camaraderie, about being a family. Her earlier defensiveness about needing to feel like she was pulling her own weight made more sense to him now, too. He was slowly breaking down that wall and, he hoped, gaining her trust in the process.

"I see," Tommy said with a frown. He would understand the implications of her life better than anyone. "She sounds like a strong woman."

Joshua nodded. On the outside? She was tough. But she'd constructed a fortress around her heart. It took a lot of strength to walk away from her boys in order to throw everything she had into finding Isabel and he could see that decision hadn't come lightly by the depths in her blue eyes. It took sheer determination and grit to do what she was doing. And that was one of the many reasons he wanted to do everything he could to help. "We better not keep her waiting."

Joshua led Tommy into the guest room where Alice waited. Her hands were clasped, resting on her lap. The bandage wrapped in gauze covered her entire right forearm.

"Thank you for agreeing to see me, Ms. Green," Tommy said after introductions.

"Call me Alice." Her body language, clasped hands and tension lines creasing her forehead, said that she was not at ease.

Ryder appeared in the doorway. "Whatever's going on, I want in."

Joshua would remind his brother that he was in no condition to help catch a guy like Perez if it would do any good. It wouldn't. So, he said, "I'll get another chair."

By the time he returned, Tommy was sitting in the guest chair, leaned slightly forward with his torso angled toward Alice. Joshua set the kitchen chair down next to Tommy and then sat on the foot of the bed.

"First off, I wanted to thank you for what you did on-site," Tommy began.

"Anyone in this room would do the same for me," she countered with a glance toward Ryder.

Joshua had noticed she didn't like receiving compliments. He needed to change that. She should know how brave everyone thought she was. And strong. *And beautiful*, that annoying little voice in the back of his head said again. Annoying or not, the voice was right. Even banged up and defensive she was beautiful.

"I'd take you on my team any day," Tommy said, the comment making the tension lines bracketing her mouth ease. That was the best compliment a cop could receive.

"Thank you, Sheriff," she said and then changed the subject. "Have you figured out what that map is about?"

"We can talk about the map in a second. I appreciate what you did for Ryder. He's more like a brother to me than a friend so I owe you. I was also thanking you for making the call to the sheriff before you set the station wagon on fire," he said.

"I don't know what you're talking about." Alice moved her right arm to her side as though shielding it from Tommy's view would make him not notice it. And that's exactly how Joshua knew she was guilty. He'd been so grateful that she'd helped Ryder that he hadn't really thought about much else.

Tommy leaned closer. "I'm not condemning you for setting the fire. I might've done the same thing given what you were up against if I'd thought of it. In case I haven't made myself clear, I'm grateful that you did whatever was necessary to save my friend."

Alice had believed it was Joshua in there and from the looks of it she'd been willing to sacrifice herself to save him. He shouldn't be surprised. She'd been doing the same thing for Isabel even though she was putting herself in grave danger doing so and she'd done it for him when she realized Perez would be after him. He'd find a way to convince her to stay on the sidelines and let law enforcement do their jobs. Or he'd do it himself. No way was he allowing her to risk her life anymore.

"What makes you so sure it was me who made the call?" She wasn't exactly denying it.

"Because dispatch received an anonymous call before the fire was set based on the preliminary report from the fire marshal. He chalked it up to a computer glitch or human error, thinking the time stamp was wrong on the call. You know what I think?"

Alice didn't respond but she suddenly became very interested in a patch of blanket on her lap.

Joshua put his hand on her leg to offer some measure of reassurance.

"You phoned it in right before you lit that fire," Tommy continued. "I'm guessing you were already injured and you figured you might not have time to call once everything was in motion."

"They had Joshua, or so I thought, and it was only a matter of time before Perez's men killed him," she admitted. "I didn't know how long that would take. They'd try to get information out of him first and I knew for certain he wasn't about to give them any, which would anger them and probably speed up the whole process. I couldn't live with his blood on my hands since he got into this mess trying to help me in the first place."

Ryder pushed up to his feet, walked to the bed, and hugged her. "Thank for saving me but especially because you thought you were saving my brother."

Alice awkwardly hugged him back with her one good arm before bowing her head and wiping her eye. Joshua was pretty certain she'd just tried to hide tears. He gently squeezed her calf where his fingers rested, ignoring the electricity pulsing up his arm from contact.

She glanced at him and he was pretty certain her cheeks flushed and that didn't exactly help with his inappropriate attraction to her.

"So what now?" she asked, clearly needing to change the subject.

"I made contact with the task force and offered my resources to the team," Tommy said, throwing her a lifeline.

One that sank to the ocean floor instead of floating.

"That's all?" Her stress levels had just spiked

based on the anger thinning her lips and her tense expression.

"You of all people know that I have to follow protocol. The good news is that after looking at the property on the map and realizing it's in my county we have a good chance they'll take me up on my offer," he added quickly.

That seemed to strike a chord with Alice although she stopped short of relaxing. Joshua already knew how much she distrusted the task force. He also knew they'd warned her to stay out of their investigation and he didn't want to think about the fact that he might be killing his own chances for a job with the FBI by associating with this case.

"Until we know what's inside that house, I can't do much of anything," Tommy said honestly.

"Do you know the area very well?" she asked.

"Yes. Most of the folks are decent and like to keep to themselves. That's why they buy an acre of land because they want space between themselves and their neighbors," Tommy said. "The house itself is small but there are several barns on the site and that could be used to hold victims."

"Have you sent a deputy to canvass the neighbors yet?" she asked.

"That's the easiest way to get myself excluded from the investigation, so the answer is no."

Alice blew out a breath and she looked completely at a loss. "What's the next step then?"

"Wait until I hear back from the leader of the task force. Get myself included in the process."

"Isabel could be long gone by the time they act," Alice said, more than a hint of hopelessness in her voice.

"We won't give up until we find her," Joshua said and Ryder quickly chimed in with his pledge.

"I'm going to pretend I didn't hear that," Tommy said on a harsh sigh. "I know this is asking a lot but I need a commitment from all three of you to give this a little time."

"There's no—"

"What? Time to do this the right way?" Tommy stopped her. "Let me put it this way. You may rush in and save Isabel but what then? Perez is still on the loose. All three of you are constantly looking over your shoulder and I already know that you're going to tell me that's okay. You don't mind making the sacrifice to find someone you obviously love so much. But here's the kicker. Perez is still out there because the entire operation was botched. Other girls are still being taken, girls like Isabel. They're being ripped from their lives and their families destroyed all because you ran out of patience."

Tears streamed down Alice's cheeks but she didn't make a move to clear them or speak. Tommy's words were obviously scoring a direct hit.

"I don't mean to sound harsh, or maybe I do. There's a big picture here that we can't lose sight of even though I understand your reasoning one hundred percent. Perez has to be stopped because he is ruining lives. And if that means I have to shout from the rooftops or remind you every day, I will. If I have to get down on my knees and beg you to take a step back, I'll do it. He's a monster and he belongs behind bars where he can't hurt any more girls." Tommy stood and started pacing. "I don't even have to remind you guys that if anyone tied to this case sees Alice so much as park her car on the same block as a stakeout she'll be arrested on the spot, which will do Isabel absolutely no good."

No one spoke for several long minutes that stretched on, even though Joshua knew that his friend was right. Joshua moved to the window, and cracked open the curtain, flooding the room with natural light.

"You won't get any interference from me," Alice finally said. "But I want your word that you'll keep me posted every step of the way. Anything happens, even something you think means nothing, I want to know about it."

"Deal," Tommy said without hesitation, which seemed to ease some of Alice's anxiety. "And since I know you won't be able to walk away completely, I want the same courtesy."

"I'll touch base with my informant and see if I can squeeze him for more information about possible routes or what the compound might be used for," she said motioning toward her cell. "I'll let you know if I get anything out of him."

"Sounds like a plan." Tommy glanced from Ryder to Joshua. "Are we good?"

"We're all on the same side," Joshua said as Ryder nodded. "We want to put an end to Perez's operation."

"I'll text the minute I hear from the task force," Tommy said, and then moved toward the door.

"I'll walk him out," Ryder said, pushing to his feet.

"We need to fix up that arm," Joshua said to Alice, moving the tray table filled with supplies next to the bed.

She was already picking at the tape holding her gauze together with her left hand.

"I can do that," Joshua said quickly.

When she looked up, there were tears streaming down her face.

"What is it? What's wrong?" he asked, taking a seat on the bed next to her. He leaned to the right placing his weight on his fisted hands on either side of her thighs. "You can talk to me."

She turned to face the opposite wall. "I'm just frustrated that's all."

There was more to it than that. He could read her pretty well by now. But she still seemed determined not to let him in.

ALICE'S BOYS WERE in Tucson, safe. Isabel was out there somewhere, in trouble. Alice was stuck in a bed, wounded. This wasn't the life she'd envisioned for the people she loved. And the worst part about the whole situation was how helpless she felt. She picked at the corner of the medical tape. It didn't budge. She yanked at it, ripping the gauze instead of the tape. *Great.* She couldn't even do that right.

"Let me help," Joshua soothed. His masculine tone offered more comfort than she knew better to take.

"I need to make the call to my informant that I promised the sheriff," she countered, reaching for her cell on the nightstand next to the bed.

"It can wait until I'm finished." He shot her

a look that begged the question of why she was being so difficult.

Relaxing and being "helped" wasn't exactly her forte. She'd never been a spa-day girl. She'd rather poke her eyes out than get a massage although Joshua's hands on her felt pretty damn good. Her body hummed with awareness every time he got close enough to reach out and touch. So, she did reach out for him just to see what it did to her body.

With her left hand she grabbed a fistful of his black V-neck and pulled him toward her. Her arm might be burned and her side stabbed but there was nothing wrong with her lips and right now she wanted to kiss the cowboy more than she wanted to breathe. She pressed her mouth against his, briefly, and then pulled back to check his reaction.

Big mistake looking into those deep green eyes this close. They opened slowly and a flash of primal need registered before he spoke.

"This a good idea?" he asked, that spark growing into something more flaming.

"Probably not but I don't care." She pressed her lips to his again, need rising from low in her belly and sending warmth to that feminine spot between her thighs.

The cowboy's tongue surged inside her mouth and she parted her lips, ready for more.

His fingers cradled the base of her neck and she lost herself in the moment. His mouth moving against hers, their tongues tangled, and all she could think about was how much she wanted more.

And then he pulled back. He stared into her eyes daring her to speak.

She didn't.

"I need to change your bandage," he said.

"Did I do something wrong?" Her heart pounded against her ribs and her breathing had become a little frantic in those few seconds their mouths fused.

"We don't need this distraction right now."

Was that how he classified what was simmering between them since they'd met? *A distraction.* At least she knew where she stood with Joshua O'Brien.

Alice stuck out her burned arm and looked the other way while he grabbed the container of salve that looked like white cupcake frosting and then smoothed the cream over her blistered skin. When he was finished dressing her wound, he handed her a pair of ibuprofen and a glass of water.

"You can take more than two of these according to the doc," he said and his voice was low and gravelly.

She tried to ignore that fact.

"Two's fine," she said, thinking how much she needed to check on her twins, to hear their little coos. As soon as Joshua left the room, she'd make the call. In the meantime, she took the pills from his opened palm, ignoring the fissures of heat the contact brought. Lot of good those did her. Apparently, the need to act on their attraction was one-sided.

"If you need anything, I'll be in the shower," he said, adding, "a very cold shower."

Alice couldn't hold back a smile as she watched him walk out of the room, checking out the ripple of muscles down his back through his T-shirt.

Maybe it was out-of-control hormones or the fact that she hadn't had sex in longer than she cared to admit, but Joshua O'Brien was probably the sexiest man she'd ever met.

Once he cleared the room she phoned her neighbor who was watching the boys. Marla picked up on the first ring.

"How are my babies?" Alice asked, forcing cheer in her voice she didn't feel.

"Wonderful. Let me round them up and I'll put them on," Marla said.

Alice ignored the stab of pain in her chest that had nothing to do with her injuries and everything to do with missing her boys. She could hear sounds of them laughing in the background and an image of Marla chasing them around the living room instead of her doing it sent another shard of pain through her chest. Their given names might be Alex and Andrew but she should've named them Rowdy and Rambunctious, and she missed everything about them both.

"Hel-low?" Rambunctious, aka Andrew, got on the line first.

"Hi, baby," Alice said, loving the sound of his little voice.

"M-m-momma!" he exclaimed.

"Are you being a good boy for Miss Marla?" she asked, knowing full well her boys were energetic angels. Having a retired school teacher as a neighbor had been a godsend. Marla's only child had a job overseas and her husband's health was failing, so she'd needed to stick close to home. She'd offered to take care of the boys to help Alice, but also because she missed her own grandchildren.

"Uh-huh," Rambunctious said. His heavy breaths from crawling around coupled with his sheer excitement vibrated across the line.

"I love you, Andrew," she said, fighting tears, figuring she'd held his attention about as long as he could.

Rowdy popped on to the line next and she could hear shuffling noises, and bare feet on

Marla's tile floors as Rambunctious belly-laughed in the background. Was he walking? No, she didn't want to know. It did no good to know what she was missing out on. Knowing wouldn't bring Isabel back faster.

Alice sighed. She missed those belly laughs.

"Momma?" he said in his adorable baby talk.

"That's right, baby. It's me."

His burst of excitement nearly crushed her heart. She heard something that sounded like the phone being dropped before Marla's voice returned to the line.

"All is well here," she said, recovering quickly.

Alice needed that. She desperately needed to know that her boys were okay. She needed someone else, too, as scary as it was to admit that fact. He was currently in a cold shower in the other room and she'd probably just ruined their friendship by kissing him.

"How are you?" Marla asked.

"I'll be better when this whole ordeal is over and I can come home," she said on a sigh.

After chatting about bedtimes and activities for several minutes, Alice ended the call having safely avoided the topic of how she was really doing. With two boys less than a year old in tow, Marla didn't have time for lengthy conversations and Alice was grateful for that fact. She'd broken down in tears enough in the past twenty-four hours to last a lifetime and she'd never been much of a crier.

Next, she called Dale, hoping her informant might know something about the address on the map. She was getting restless sitting in bed while everyone else worked on the case. Doing nothing, being alone with her thoughts was the worst feeling. She needed to keep her mind busy.

The call rolled straight into voice mail.

ALL THINGS CONSIDERED, Joshua figured the meeting with Tommy had gone well. After dressing Alice's burns like the doc had trained him to do he decided to return to the trailer site so he could survey the area. At least that was the excuse he used to get out of the house. Being with Alice 24/7 was messing with his mind. He needed to get some fresh air to clear his head, but his thoughts kept winding back to that kiss. The softness of her lips. How much he wanted to kiss that little dimple on the corner of her mouth to the left.

He dismissed it as dangerous. Joshua couldn't afford the slightest slip right now. Too much was on the line with people he cared about, not to mention his own life. He could chalk this attraction up to primal need in a life-and-death situation but it was more than that. There was so much more to Alice than a physical attraction and that stirred his heart in ways he didn't want to think about while he was about to make a serious life change. Momentarily being trapped in a life he didn't want wasn't the best time to let his emotions run wild. The best thing he could do for both of them was redirect his thoughts to the case.

It played to Joshua's hand that Perez believed he was dead. Even so, he planned to have a conversation with Ryder about staying at the ranch until Perez was safely out of town. In the meantime both needed to keep a low profile, which was why Joshua had borrowed Dr. McConnell's pickup truck rather than take his own Jeep. In this part of the country, there were more pickups and SUVs than sedans on the road, so it was the best way to blend in.

A cold front had blown through and it was too chilly outside for Joshua's taste. One of the best parts about leaving Colorado for Texas was gaining sunshine and warmth. Nature wasn't cooperating with his plans today. He buttoned up his denim jacket, tucked his chin to his chest and adjusted his gray Stetson low on his forehead as he made his way through the brush, retracing his steps from yesterday. There could be feds on-site or staking out the place to see if one of the criminals returned so he needed to stay alert.

While he'd expected crime scene tape cordoning off the place, he didn't anticipate seeing deputies and feds crawling everywhere. He couldn't risk getting closer to the single wide, so he retreated and placed a call to Tommy once he was back in McConnell's pickup.

"Did you connect with the task force?" he asked as soon as Tommy answered, hoping there was some good news to come out of this.

"I just sent over the map and Ms. Green's statement," he replied with a questioning overtone to his voice. "Do I need to ask why?"

"You didn't reveal her identity, did you?" Joshua asked.

"It's best that they know she's cooperating. They'll go easier on her," Tommy said.

He was right so Joshua let it go.

"I'm at the crime scene and the place is crawling with law enforcement. You have any idea what that's about?" Joshua asked, trying not to think about just how badly he could be blowing his chances at ever working for the FBI if he was caught interfering with a federal investigation.

"No, I don't." Tommy paused for a beat. "I don't have to tell you not to stick around, do I?"

"I'm on my way back to McConnell's," Joshua

said, turning the key over in the ignition. "Think you can find out what's going on?"

"Can't make any promises they'll tell me, but it never hurts to ask."

The call from Tommy came a few minutes before McConnell was due back for lunch. Ryder joined Joshua in Alice's room as he put the call on speaker.

"I have bad news so I'll cut to the chase," Tommy said. "A body was found inside the trailer."

Being able to identify one of Perez's men could go a long way toward cracking this case open. There were a few knowns, so Joshua hoped this wasn't a no-lead. "I'm guessing it's too early to have a positive ID on the body."

"No. We got it."

"How is that possible?" Joshua asked. "I figured with the fire—"

"Because he wasn't burned at all. He was stabbed through the throat and his tongue had been cut off," Tommy said wearily. "He was found in the living room with his wallet in his pocket. Does the name Dale Sanders mean anything?"

Alice's face paled. "He's my informant."

Joshua could almost read Alice's thoughts because they would be similar to his own if roles were reversed. Dale might've been tangled up with criminals and dependent on drugs but no one deserved to die and especially not like this. Dale had to have had a mother or someone who loved him—even if it was misguided love which was often the case with people who lived outside the law—out there somewhere and her heart would be broken with the news.

"This is obviously an attempt to shut Alice up or warn her to back off," Joshua said. Stabbing someone was incredibly personal and a bigger message couldn't be sent than by cutting someone's tongue out. The crime was violent and meant to show just how betrayed Perez felt by Sanders.

"It's his signature," Alice said, all color draining from her face. "It's what he does to men in his organization who turn on him. I've seen this same scenario with one of his top lieutenants who also happened to be his nephew."

"Damn," Joshua said. The word was followed by silence. "I'm sorry this happened to your informant. And I know it's a blow to the investigation but we can recover. The feds are most likely working the other angle, right, Tommy?"

It seemed coldhearted to focus attention on the investigation but that's what he needed to do. Processing Dale's death would take time.

"They're setting up a raid as we speak, figuring they need to move fast. If Perez thinks his operation has a hole in it they fear he might clean out the compound."

"So they're going in tonight?" Alice asked with as hopeful a voice as Joshua figured she could muster under the circumstances.

"It might take a couple of days to coordinate and organize but they don't want to wait any longer than they have to since the guys tried to set fire to the trailer to erase evidence. We know they'll do the same thing to the compound if they realize there could be a threat to that location. Also, a print was lifted at the scene. It belonged to Perez so we can link him to the crimes committed there now."

"About time we got some good news in this case," Joshua said. "Also good that the feds are moving quickly. If Isabel's there, they'll find her."

Joshua knew full well that the teen could be anywhere by now. Six weeks was a long time to be missing with a man like Perez.

"I'll let you know everything as it unfolds," Tommy said. "I know this is difficult but sit tight a little longer. We're getting close."

Joshua thanked Tommy before ending the call.

"I'll join you in the kitchen to make a fresh

pot of coffee in a minute," Joshua said to Ryder. His brother took the hint and moved out of the room.

"What is it, Alice? What are you thinking?" he asked, moving to her side and then taking her left hand in his. This wasn't the time to think about how small hers seemed by comparison. Or how much contact with her brought warmth to his chest like he'd never known.

She blinked and a few tears rolled down her cheeks.

"What is it?" Joshua asked, and then it dawned on him.

"If they tortured Dale, and I'm sure they did, he probably told them about me looking for Isabel…"

"And blew your cover," Joshua added.

"Worse than that, he just signed her death warrant."

Chapter Nine

Alice pushed the plate of food to the back of the tray and focused on the glass of iced tea, tracing the rim with her left index finger. It had been three nights since they'd heard word from Tommy and she was tired of everyone reminding her that was a good thing. Experience had taught her that just because they hadn't found a body—and she meant Isabel's—didn't mean they wouldn't. Her mind snapped to the past, to her mother. She couldn't think about the fact that she was putting her life in danger, which could leave the twins without a mother or father, in order to help someone else. A new person had taken over the task force at the FBI. She needed to press Tommy for a name. He wasn't giving any other details.

"You planning to eat any of that or just stare it down all night?" Joshua asked from the doorway, startling her.

Ever since that kiss and the awkwardness that had followed she was unnerved by his presence.

"How long have you been standing there?" she asked, forking a piece of broccoli.

"Long enough to know that your food is getting cold." He leaned against the doorjamb, filling the frame. "Mind if I come in? It's time to replace your bandage."

Alice nodded, not especially thrilled about the prospect of slathering more of that silver sulfadiazine onto her skin. The first couple of days it had been manna from heaven, somehow magically pulling out the heat from the burn while soothing her patches of varying shades of red. The blisters came on day two, popped on day three and now large parts of her skin alternately oozed and bled. The cream burned when a new coat was put on and her ibuprofen barely touched the pain but she needed a clear head so she refused to take more than two pills at a time. She'd finally agreed to a cold compress and that had given her a few hours of sleep last night. Dr. McConnell had offered reassurances that Alice was healing beautifully. She would have to take the good doctor's word for it.

The mattress dipped under Joshua's weight as he positioned the folding tray with supplies next to him. It didn't help that he'd avoided spending time in her room since the kiss and she wondered if he regretted ever getting mixed up with her. Alice was like a virus, dangerous to everyone including the host.

Wow. What was up with the self-pity, Green?

She winced as the cowboy pulled the non-stick pad away from her arm.

"Sorry," she said quickly.

"Don't be." His calm voice was a welcome change to silence. "I hate that I'm hurting you."

"Only way to make it better, right?" She said, forcing a laugh. There were about five shades of red on her arm. The first-degree burns were starting to heal thanks to the magic cream. Those were pale pink. The area where the two-by-two-inch blister had popped was level five red. So red, in fact, it almost looked burgundy.

"I spoke to Tommy a few minutes ago," he said.

"Oh, yeah? Any news?" she asked, grateful to have something to focus on besides the pain. In times like these she reminded herself that it could be so much worse.

"They've had the compound under surveillance long enough to assess the situation."

"And that is?" Impatience edged her tone.

"The place is being used as a holding cell. The horse barns are where they believe girls are being held and possibly drugged, although no one knows the last part for sure," he added. "No one has tried to escape so they're bound by something."

"So the place is a major component of their overall operation," she said, grateful for progress.

"Yes, and the feds believe there's evidence there that can tie Perez to the location."

"Like what?" she asked.

"Computer entries. They received a tip from one of their informants that Perez keeps an 'inventory' log and likes to be updated daily about his 'cargo.'" He smoothed the frosting-like cream over her burns.

"I don't care what the informant thinks. Perez is smart enough to cover his tracks," she said and she couldn't help but think about Dale.

"All they need is a link to an IP for one of his devices and they can tie him to the crimes," he said. "He also has a lieutenant in his operation who is questioning tactics, according to another source. The feds think they can get him to turn on Perez by offering witness protection."

"If that's the case then prosecutors will have enough to work with." She didn't ask about where this would leave Isabel. If Alice could get ahold of those records, she could find out for herself. Getting to know the leader of the task force was even more important now.

"They were able to get enough intel to get a warrant to search the place. Illegal activity is occurring on that site and that can't be denied. Seizing the computers should give us the data needed to link the operation to Perez and nail his coffin closed for a lot of years," Joshua said.

"*If* everything goes according to plan." She knew a man like Perez would most likely have a fail-safe in place and that was the reason he was still at large, kidnapping girls and getting away with it among other heinous crimes. He knew how to be involved in day-to-day operations while keeping a safe distance. But if there was a chance she could get Isabel back she wouldn't argue and she sure didn't want the task force to wait. "How do they know about the girls in the barn?"

"They were able to use a drone to obtain footage of a truckload of girls being carried out of the back of a semi and into the main barn."

"Did they get a positive ID on any of the girls?" she asked, a spark of hope lighting up inside her chest. She quickly suppressed it, afraid to give the emotion too much credence. Hope could be more dangerous than fear.

"Yes, there's a positive ID on one of the girls, Erin Daily. She was reported missing from a wealthy Dallas suburb two days ago," he said. "One of the girls being carried inside fit her description down to the clothes she was wearing at the time of her disappearance."

She didn't ask about Isabel because if Joshua had news he would've come right out with it.

"When is the raid?" she asked.

"Tommy couldn't say for sure. The team doesn't want to risk a leak so they're being tight-lipped about it. He did guess that they'd be going sometime tomorrow and possibly at first light."

Once Joshua applied a thick layer of salve and a fresh bandage covered by gauze, he made a move to get up.

"Can I ask another question?" Alice was trying to build her courage, which was faltering at the moment.

"Okay."

"In your professional opinion, what are the chances Isabel is there?" she asked.

"I wish I had a number, but I don't." He moved toward the door. "You need an extra blanket tonight? The cold front isn't planning to let up and they say it might freeze."

"No. I'm good." She pushed off her covers.

"Where are you headed?" he asked.

"I was just going to put the tray up. I'm not hungry right now," she said.

"I'll do that for you." He waved her off before taking the tray and disappearing down the hall.

Alice leaned against the headboard and pulled her knees up, trying to push the raid from her thoughts. If Isabel had come through the compound there was a good chance that she had already been moved to another location.

A GUST OF cold wind blasted, causing branches to scrape against the window outside Alice's bedroom. Restless, she pushed off the covers. Sleep was as close as summer and she was about to give up hope when a figure appeared in her doorway.

"You okay?" Joshua asked.

She hugged her knees into her chest, not exactly sure how to answer that question. Physically, she was fine, healing. Mentally, she was sick with worry. Instead of a real answer, she mumbled that she'd get over it.

She expected Joshua to turn and walk away, like he had been doing. But he walked toward her, sat next to her on the bed, and covered her hands with his.

"Waiting stinks. Not knowing what's going on when you're used to being in the action is even worse," he said, his masculine voice warming her. "I can't even begin to imagine what it must be like to be away from your boys this long. And then to be uncertain about what is happening with Isabel on top of it all is pretty rough."

He nailed her frustration and feelings of inadequacy, leaving out the part about what was going on between them adding extra confusion into the mix.

"I'm sorry about what happened to Dale," he added. "I know that must be bugging you, too."

She couldn't even begin to process the thought of being responsible for his death.

"You're going through a lot and your injuries have you sidelined," he said, pretty much nailing it again.

"No one will ever accuse me of having too much patience," she joked, trying to lighten the tension. But it was true. "The truth is that all this worry is driving me insane."

"What can I do to help?" he asked.

She could see well enough in the darkness to know he was being sincere based on his expression. She surprised herself when she said, "I know that you're not…*interested*…in starting anything and that's fine. I agree that it's not a good idea. It's just… I don't want to be alone right now. Stay with me tonight."

The long pause he issued made her think twice about her request. If he really didn't want to be around her that much she shouldn't push him.

"Okay," he said and she noticed how gruff his voice had become.

Alice curled up on her side under the covers, facing the opposite wall as he climbed in next to her. The next thing she knew he pulled her toward him and repositioned her so that her head was on his chest and she rested in the crook of his arm. For the first time in a long time, she relaxed against a strong, muscled body with warm, soft skin pressed against hers.

Alice closed her eyes and fell into a deep sleep.

Sunlight filled the room as Alice blinked awake. Her legs were entwined with Joshua's and she could hear his even breathing, feel the rhythm of his heartbeat as it matched hers.

Neither had moved much from last night and she wasn't sure how long she'd been awake when he surprised her by tightening his arms around her. He pulled her in close and pressed a kiss to her forehead so fluidly it was like he'd done the same thing every morning for their entire lives.

And then he seemed to catch himself because his grip loosened and he cleared his throat.

"How long have you been awake?" he asked.

"Not long." She hadn't exactly checked the clock. She'd been content to lie there in his arms, which should freak her out. Somehow, it calmed her instead. She reasoned that with everything going on it could've been anyone in that bed next to her and she would've felt reassured. It was a lie. She gave herself a free pass in the honesty department this morning.

"You must be hungry. You barely touched your dinner last night." He eased his arm out from underneath her and then sat up, rubbing his eyes. She tried not to stare at the ripples of muscles on his back visible through the white T-shirt he wore.

There was no way she was embarrassing herself by throwing herself at him again even though she wanted to do just that.

"I can get breakfast," she said, tossing the covers aside.

"Hold on there." His hand on her calf stopped her and it also sent a current rippling up her leg.

He didn't immediately speak even though it seemed like there was something on his mind.

Before he could make some lame excuse as to why last night couldn't happen again, she said, "Thanks for...you know...everything. I haven't slept that well in a long time."

Getting too comfortable with Joshua O'Brien would be a mistake. Alice didn't have to be a rocket scientist to figure out that as soon as this case was over she would go back to her normal life in Tucson with Isabel—she prayed—and her boys, and he would go back to life on his family's ranch.

"Me, either," he said, and that shocked her. What problems did he have to keep him awake at night? "I'll put on a pot of coffee."

He didn't immediately make a move to get up.

"Are you okay?" she asked, concerned.

"I need a few minutes. Waking up with a beautiful woman in your arms does...*something* to a man."

Alice's cheeks flushed and heat washed over her. All she could say was, "Oh."

"Go ahead and start without me," he said. "I'll be there in a minute."

Alice couldn't think of a snappy comeback, so she moved into the bathroom to brush her teeth before heading into the kitchen. She pulled a carton of fresh eggs from the fridge at about the same time she heard the shower turn on in the other room. Her lips curled into a smile knowing the effect she'd had on him. It felt good to know that she was still considered an attractive woman and he wasn't completely immune to her.

There wasn't much she could make in the

way of breakfast food except for a mean omelet and toast. She went to her go-to meal, stirring milk into the beaten eggs. She chopped an onion and cut a green bell pepper, tossing both in the pan with the eggs. Moments before the omelet was perfect she added shredded cheddar cheese just long enough to melt it.

"What smells so good?" he asked, entering the room as the toaster popped.

Another smile broke on Alice's face, a rare occurrence since Isabel's disappearance.

He walked over, placed his hand on her hip and a kiss on her forehead. "How are you really holding up?"

"I can use a little extra glue to be honest. I'm scared," she admitted as she turned off the heat and set the pan off the red coils.

ALICE'S ADMISSION SURPRISED JOSHUA. Something—and he still wasn't sure what—had changed between them in the past three days that had allowed Alice to lower her guard. He didn't want to get too inside his head about the transformation, or admit how much he liked it.

She leaned into him, and he could feel her trembling—not from fear but from something else—as he pulled her into his arms.

Much more of this and he'd need another cold shower.

"I don't know about you but I could use a strong cup of coffee." The feelings he was beginning to have for Alice were a distraction he couldn't afford no matter how much his body said otherwise. One call from the FBI and he'd be out of there. It would take a little while to finish his application so he could see this case through, which most likely wouldn't be too much longer after the big break they'd received when Alice had found that address. But then, he didn't need to get ahead of himself with the FBI. It was a lengthy process and he hadn't been called in for an interview yet.

"Sounds like a plan," she said, turning to plate the eggs.

The smell of bacon replaced the scent of her shampoo, a mix of citrus, flowers and the sun. As much as he loved bacon, and he did love bacon, her scent was so much better.

He made coffee before fishing his cell from his pocket and placing it on the table alongside two steaming mugs.

"What do we do now?" She plunged her fork into her omelet.

"We eat."

Chapter Ten

Joshua's cell phone buzzed and Alice's heart jumped into her throat. She glanced at the clock. It was half past one and they'd just sat down to lunch, which she had no appetite for.

"It's Tommy," he said, glancing up from the screen.

Alice set her glass of water on the table as he answered the call.

"I'm putting you on speaker with me and Alice," Joshua said into the receiver.

After perfunctory greetings, Tommy said, "I'll share everything I know. The raid went down two hours ago after the task force received a tip that an empty semi was on its way to the compound for a pickup. The team mobilized quickly into their white minivan two miles from the site. A chopper full of feds took to the air. The plan was to drop in from above while ground troops engaged. There were a dozen law enforcement officers on scene, two of which were my deputies and another pair from our neighbors in Hampstead County. There were four agents from the Bureau of Alcohol, Tobacco, Firearms and Explosives, and another four from the FBI."

"Sounds like they brought enough firepower to the fight," Joshua said as Alice held her breath waiting for the news she desperately wanted to hear. Alice also thought about the fact that so much could go wrong when officers from varying agencies pulled together so quickly without time to rehearse and get to know each other's habits when going on a raid. It was a fact that could prove fatal when the pressure was on. Knowing each other intimately, who went right and who went left on instinct could mean the difference between walking out alive and mistakes being made, critical mistakes like an officer being shot by another officer. It was always a risk with task forces but especially ones that didn't have a chance to get to know each other and rehearse. Yes, there were fail-safes in place with plans made accordingly, but under pressure people tended to revert to their comfort zone.

"Eighteen girls with an estimated age range of twelve to sixteen years old were found inside the residence and the primary barn. Ziploc bags containing pills or a powdery material were also discovered and the substance inside is believed to be ketamine."

Alice's heart pounded against her ribs and sadness pushed through. So many lives affected. So much innocence lost. In order to be able to deal with situations like this and still do her job well, Alice had learned to compartmentalize her emotions, to hold them at bay. She'd learned to deal with them after her adrenaline spike was a distant memory and she was alone in her bed. The avalanche came when the rest of the world was quiet. And, sometimes, the weight was crushing.

Rather than allow herself to be sucked under, she refocused her energy on the girls, on Isabel, and how all of them needed everyone in law enforcement to keep a clear head. "Do any of the girls match Isabel's description?"

There was a pause, which pretty much gave Alice her answer.

"I'm sorry," Tommy said quietly.

Joshua was already standing behind her. His hands on her shoulders were the only things keeping her from unraveling.

"What about the computers? Surely, they can track her if the records were kept up to date like you said before." She couldn't suppress the panicked feelings engulfing her so she didn't try. Instead, she channeled them into crystal-clear thinking and pure determination. Perez would pay. She didn't know how or when, but he would not be allowed to hurt other innocent children.

"That's the hope," Tommy said and she could tell he was trying not to get her hopes up in case the files were too encrypted. "The FBI has them on a plane to Quantico, but then you already know that."

"And Perez? Any chance he was around during the raid?" Joshua asked.

"He disappeared without a trace, but the feds have a couple of his men," Tommy said. "Garcia got a visual on Perez. There was heavy gunfire and he disappeared in the chaos."

"Were any of our guys hurt?" Alice immediately asked.

"An agent and one of my deputies volunteered to go in first. Both were injured in the hailstorm. They've been taken to Bluff General Hospital for treatment."

"I'm sorry to hear that," Joshua said and Alice was about to say the same thing. Again, her heart hurt but she couldn't allow the emotions to take center stage. Not with so many other lives at stake.

"Garcia is in critical but stable condition for

now. The federal officer was treated and released," Tommy said.

There was a moment of silence on the line in a show of respect.

Hopelessness was settling over Alice. Two good men were down, her informant was gone, and Perez was free. Isabel was still out there and most likely had been sold given that she wasn't at the compound. Of course, this might not be the only holding place. Although, given the number of girls being kept there it probably was. Finding Isabel just got a thousand times more complicated.

"What about Hammond? Did you get him?" Alice asked, praying they picked up the guy who was believed to be ready to roll on Perez.

Tommy's delay in answering was another blow.

"He was shot."

"Fatally?" she asked.

"I don't want to give you false hope. He's still in surgery and the doctor won't have answers until he's out."

So, no Perez. No Isabel. And the only person the feds had a decent chance of rolling might not make it out of surgery.

"What else?" Joshua said when Alice was unable to keep probing.

"That's all the bad news, and it's a lot," Tommy

said. "Here's some good news. Teams are combing the site and they have all been briefed on what Isabel looks like."

Not exactly good news but Alice would take what she could get. At least law enforcement was working on her side again.

"I offered my interrogation room and holding cells for the few men who were placed under arrest. And the task force is taking me up on it," Tommy added.

That was better. At least Tommy would be in the loop now. And Alice had every intention of being in the adjoining room, staring through that one-way mirror during those interviews.

Joshua squeezed her shoulders so he must've been thinking the same thing.

"And the best news is that we have two still-sedated but coherent girls who have been treated and who are being brought in for questioning. Again, I offered my private office."

Alice jumped to her feet and shot a look at Joshua that said she was going down to that station no matter who tried to stop her.

He nodded.

"We'll be right there, Sheriff," Alice said.

"That's not advi—"

"Either way, I'm coming," she said matter-of-factly. He could argue until the cows came home but she was going to be in that room.

"Perez is still out there," Tommy started.

"I'll bring her, Tommy. I can get her there safely," Joshua said.

"Need I remind you that he and his men will shoot both of you on sight?" There was genuine concern in Tommy's voice and Alice appreciated there being two people she could count on to have her back. She missed the camaraderie since going out on her own.

"He won't get anywhere near the town right now," Joshua reasoned. "Not with all this heat."

"Normally, I'd agree with you but this guy is trouble. It would be exactly like him to set up near the station just to make sure his guys don't talk," Tommy said. "I have all my people on extra alert but you need to stay put and wait for me to get back to you. Plus, I don't have a guarantee the feds won't arrest Alice for obstruction. I'm working on it."

"I understand," Alice acquiesced, ignoring the what-the-heck look from Joshua.

"Good. Thank you. I'm not looking to make any of this worse. I'll share everything that I can from the interviews," Tommy said.

Joshua thanked his friend before ending the call. He turned his full attention to Alice. "You want to tell me what the heck that was about?"

She was already starting toward the bedroom to get dressed. "There's no use arguing with a man whose mind is already made up. Plus, I can't be sure his phone lines are secure. It's best if no one expects us, especially Perez."

"What about the possibility of being arrested?" Joshua asked.

"There's only one way to find out."

"What are you doing here?" Tommy asked as Joshua ushered Alice through the metal detector in the lobby area of the sheriff's office.

Joshua knew the layout well given that Tommy was like family and all the brothers had spent considerable time with their friend around town and visiting him in his office.

"I didn't want to explain myself over the phone but I've been tracking this case exclusively for more than six weeks now and I might be able to shed light on comments the girls make during the interview process," Alice explained. Her jaw was set and determination sparked in her eyes. "I'm here to offer my expertise as a professional consultant, that's all. You can take or leave my thoughts but I deserve to see what's going on for myself."

One of the federal agents stepped into the hallway and into view. He was short with a sturdy build. His red hair was combed to one side and almost too perfectly parted. His gaze shifted from Alice back to Joshua before narrowing. "That won't be necessary, Alice."

Joshua noted the man's posture change as he crossed his arms over his puffed-out chest. At least he wasn't reaching for handcuffs.

"I can see that you still undervalue the presence of a woman, Special Agent Fischer," Alice shot back. "What the hell are you doing here?"

What was that all about? Joshua gathered that the two already knew each other but this seemed personal. Tommy must've picked up on the animosity, too, because he excused himself to get a cup of coffee.

"This is my investigation now," Fischer said with another glance toward Joshua, and it was really more like a glare. He focused on Alice. "I need to speak to you in the other room."

"I'm here as an off-duty cop. The only people I want to listen to are beyond those walls." Alice motioned toward the back of the building where Tommy's office would be, standing her ground as she crossed her arms.

"Do I need to remind you that you aren't supposed to be involved in this investigation?" Fischer asked, his temper flaring. "All I have to do is make one phone call and you're out of a job and in jail."

"You want to arrest me? Then do it," Alice

shot back as she put her arms out, taking a page from his book. Joshua hid his smirk.

"Would you excuse us?" Fischer said to Joshua.

Before Joshua could answer, which was going to be negative unless Alice said otherwise, she was already shaking her head.

"This is not a good time, Fischer," Alice said. "We can play catch-up later. Right now, all I care about is finding out what happened to those girls."

Alice brushed past him and stalked down the hall.

"You got a problem with me?" Joshua asked Fischer directly as the man stared him down. Joshua always was one to face forward and take the bull by the horns.

"Should I?" Fischer countered.

"I don't have an issue with you unless you give me a reason," Joshua said, holding his position. Fischer had tensed and Joshua would be ready should the guy decide to throw a punch.

"You'll never be as important to her life as I will," Fischer said.

If that was true Joshua had to believe he would've known by now. And yet, her initial reaction to Fischer and their exchange sat like hot nails in Joshua's stomach. As far as Joshua could tell Fischer had no designs on Alice. Her reaction said there'd been something more than work between them. Joshua didn't like it even though he had no right to be jealous.

"That may well be but she actually wants to talk to me." Joshua walked past Fischer and straight to Tommy's office where Alice sat across from the victims. One was huddled in the other's arms with her head down. The other teen glanced up at him and immediately tensed, so he took a seat near the door as Alice offered reassurances.

Erin looked like she hadn't had a shower in days. Her long blond hair clung together in clumps against her neck, her pale blue eyes wide and frightened. She sat hunched over, avoiding eye contact with any of the males in the room. Her clothes were dirty and smelled exactly like she'd been in a barn for days. Fischer strode in still strapped to his High Horse. He stood at his full height next to where Alice sat, which was maybe five foot ten inches.

"Can you describe the men who kept you captive?" Fischer asked without a hint of empathy in his voice.

Erin's gaze dropped to the floor. She was closing up and that wasn't good. Maybe Fischer had skipped the day in witness interview techniques where they taught compassion because he was going about this all wrong. Anyone could see that Erin was intimidated by every male presence in the room, so standing over her was likely to have the exact opposite of the desired result. She closed up on his first question and he didn't seem to notice when he repeated it, louder and slower.

Then again, maybe the man wasn't thinking clearly after Alice's rebuke. Joshua got Tommy's attention and motioned for him to meet in the hallway.

"This guy isn't going to get anywhere with his tactics and he's going to hurt the investigation," Joshua started but Tommy's hand immediately came up.

"I can't interfere if that's what you're about to ask. This case belongs to the feds and if I stick my nose in they'll only cut me out." Tommy had a point.

"Granted. I know you're right but did you see her? The girl went silent the minute he stood in front of her with his chest puffed out. I don't care what's going on between him and Alice. This interview is too important to let personal…*entanglements*, for lack of a better word, taint it."

"You're right and I agree with you one hundred percent," Tommy said. "And yet my hands are still tied."

"Well, mine aren't," Joshua said, stepping

into the doorway fully aware that he was most likely about to kill his own career prospects. Seeing Erin about to cry was more than he could stand by and watch. "Special Agent Fischer, I need to speak to you in the hallway. Now."

Fischer whirled around. "If you can't see, I'm in the middle of something…"

Alice stood and placed her body in between Fischer and the girls. "I think that's a great idea. I believe the rest of these men could use a break as well. Gentlemen…"

The look Fischer shot Joshua could've covered the Sahara in a thick blanket of ice. After a quick glance at Alice, Fischer stalked toward the hall, crashing his shoulder into Joshua as he walked by. His men filed out behind him, two of whom thanked Joshua quietly on the way out. As it turned out not everyone had missed sensitivity training.

Fischer, on the other hand, was all fire and fury as he whirled around. "You pull another stunt like that and I'll make sure your SO has a full incident report for your jacket."

Joshua didn't want to think about what this might do to his current application. Even though he didn't need someone with the FBI on a hunt for his blood while he was trying to get a job with the agency, Erin didn't deserve to be placed in the middle of a different fight. Shutting the door to give Alice and the girls privacy was probably another nail in his coffin but Joshua decided to go *all in* at this point.

Agents and officers lined the walls of the hallway. The two who had thanked Joshua were the only ones standing on the same side.

Twenty minutes later, Alice emerged. "I need to go to the site."

Chapter Eleven

"There's no way I'm letting you stomp all over my crime scene," Fischer said, blocking her path. Alice was not thrilled at seeing the father of her twins. "You got your way with my witnesses now I expect a full debriefing."

"Then you can ask me anything you want at the compound because that's where I'm going," she said before turning to Tommy. "Thank you for the use of your office. The girls are exhausted so I told them to curl up on your couch and get some rest. They need to be with a woman until their parents arrive."

"I'll take care of them," an older woman with a kind face said as she stepped into the hallway. "I'm Abigail and I work for Tommy."

"I'm Alice." She quickly found herself on the receiving end of a warm hug.

"I know," Abigail said with a quick smile. "The girls are fragile right now. They need someone like you by their side," Alice said to Abigail. She straightened her shoulders to address the men again. "Someone called both of their parents, right?"

"It was the first thing I did after we positively ID'd each of them," Tommy said.

Alice didn't want to get into why it wasn't Fischer who'd made the calls but she figured it was pretty typical of him. He didn't "do" family stuff. Isn't that what he'd told her after he all but accused her of getting pregnant on purpose to derail his promotion?

Yeah, that's exactly what she'd wanted…to have her birth control fail after the two of them had been dating for all of six weeks because she didn't know that antibiotics made the pill temporarily ineffective. The long distance so-called relationship they'd had during her pregnancy was almost as big of a joke. And then, that Friday night had happened…the crowned jewel of all ways to kick off a weekend, when he'd told her that he couldn't stick around.

"Good." She lowered her voice and softened her tone when she turned to Joshua. "Will you give me a ride to the compound?"

He nodded as he fished the keys to his Jeep out of his pocket and led her toward the door before anyone could put up an argument.

Joshua didn't ask questions when he started

the engine, or when Fischer immediately hopped into his silver sedan and followed. Alice didn't like the silence or the tension sitting between them.

"We dated." That wasn't the half of it, but those were the words that blurted out of her mouth when the GPS device said they'd reached the halfway mark to their destination.

"I gathered as much," Joshua said and his tone was even, unreadable. "Is it over?"

"Yes," she said with a little more enthusiasm than she'd planned.

"He doesn't seem to realize that fact." There was a hint of jealousy in his voice now and it was confusing.

"Well, it is," she said frankly.

"Is it?" His gaze zeroed in on the stretch of road in front of them.

"For me? Absolutely," she said. "But you should know that he's technically the father of my twins."

Joshua's grip tightened on the steering wheel and his stare intensified but he didn't say a word.

ALICE COULDN'T GET a good read on Joshua since he'd been dead silent for the rest of the drive. Then there were her own stirred-up emotions to deal with about her relationship with

Joshua. Sleeping in the same bed last night, the comfort she felt in his arms, only added to her confusion. Feelings between her and Joshua complicated an already complex life. The attraction between them was strong, even he couldn't deny that now, and yet he seemed just as determined as ever not to act on it. He was smart. Alice was allowing her heart to take over common sense. She cursed her weakness and stuffed her emotions down deep, secure in the knowledge that it would never work between them.

As it was, she was lucky that she hadn't been arrested for obstruction of justice and she was pretty sure the reason Fischer had imposed himself on this case was so he could control her future. She chalked his act of chivalry up to guilt for abandoning her and the boys. As far as anything else happening between them? Fischer needed to move on. She had. Besides, how could she ever trust a man who'd walked out on her when she was at her most vulnerable?

Alice pinched the bridge of her nose trying to stem the raging headache threatening. This was going to be one red-letter day. It was also the closest she'd been to Isabel in more than six weeks. She was like a hound that'd caught a scent and she planned to follow it through to its conclusion—no matter what that meant. Erin had shared a few startling details about the way the girls had been treated. Hailey, who'd been at the compound for more than thirty terrifying days, didn't make eye contact, couldn't. Alice's heart felt ripped from her chest at seeing that girl—no older than her when she'd gone to live with the sheriff and his wife—after she'd lived through what had to have been her worst nightmare.

If that wasn't bad enough, Alice had had the added bonus of seeing Fischer again. Although, maybe she should've known he'd eventually show if only for curiosity's sake. In the first few weeks following the breakup, he'd sent checks that she'd torn up. He was only doing it out of guilt and she was determined to take care of her boys on her own, financially and otherwise. Fischer must've gotten the hint because money stopped coming a few months later and he never tried to contact her.

She had nothing to say to the man. There were no words that could smooth over the fact that he'd walked out on her when she'd needed a shoulder to lean on. The unexpected pregnancy hadn't only shaken up his world. She'd been more than shocked. And where had he been since? Her boys were about to reach their first birthday without their father. What had suddenly given Fischer a bout of conscience? If he'd wanted to see his sons he would've done it by now. Granted, if he honestly wanted to get to know his boys she wouldn't stop him. The boys deserved to know their father. But if he wanted to use them to get to her, as she suspected, he was barking up the wrong tree. Experience had taught Alice that people couldn't be trusted. Besides, her life was a confusing mess and it wouldn't be long before Joshua figured that out and disappeared, too.

The crime scene was alive with activity when Alice and Joshua arrived twenty minutes later. Neighbors in the acre lot cul-de-sac lingered at their mailboxes, heads shaking as they spoke in hushed tones. Trees lined the property as well as shrubs, making it difficult to see the house and barn from the street or neighboring houses.

"What did Erin say to you that had you needing to come here?" Joshua finally asked after parking, cutting through her heavy thoughts.

She got out and he handed her a pair of gloves and then placed a pair on his own hands. Then, he pulled a few evidence bags from the dashboard of his Jeep.

"Someone who fit Isabel's description was here when she was first brought to this place two days ago," Alice said, grateful for the change in subject. All that personal drama was making her crazy anyway.

"How certain is she?" Joshua asked. She couldn't get a good read on his emotions.

"There weren't a lot of dark-haired girls, so Isabel stood out. I asked about the birthmark on the back of her left hand. It's almost the shape of a shamrock and Erin could've sworn that she remembered something like that. She'd been so scared when she was thrown into a stall in the barn. There were men watching over the girls in shifts. They'd walk back and forth in front of the stall, checking each one, making sure the girls didn't interact or try to run," Alice said, anger rising in her chest. She knew that she should remain detached during an investigation but that was impossible in some cases and especially this one. She glanced to her right and saw a burly-looking officer removing evidence from the house while he wiped away what she figured were tears. Another had punched a board that had been nailed to a tree and used for games of darts.

Even the strongest person had a breaking point, an Achilles' heel. Heinous crimes against children were right up there at the top of the list for most officers. And especially since many of these officers were parents. The ones with daughters would be especially affected.

It would be impossible for them to completely shut out their frustration and anger. "She said that the girls were ordered to stick to their assigned corner. Erin was crying and she couldn't stop, which was drawing attention. The guards had already threatened her once, saying that if she didn't cut it out they'd pull her out and shut her up. She was afraid they'd do other things to her, too. But Isabel crawled over and held Erin until she stopped crying. She told her they would get out of there together and not to be afraid."

"Isabel sounds strong," Joshua said after a thoughtful moment and Alice was grateful they were talking again. He fell in step beside her as she walked toward the barn situated behind the ranch-style house, which teemed with law enforcement officers.

"She is. And smart. She told Erin that her mother was a cop and wouldn't stop looking until she found her." Alice's voice broke. "She was right. I won't give up until she's home."

"Neither will I," Joshua said so quietly she almost thought she'd imagined hearing it.

The barn was large enough to house a dozen horses if each were given a private stall. White paint had faded and chipped on the doors. There was straw scattered inside the individual stalls on the ground and now-empty buckets the girls had been forced to use in place of a bathroom. Erin had told Alice about all those things, the horrors of being treated worse than animals. They'd even been branded with a small capital *P* on their left hip so that buyers would know they were getting authentic Perez "product." It was sickening and Alice wanted to see the man rot in a cell for the rest of his life.

"Isabel was bought the day after Erin arrived," she finally told Joshua as they scanned the makeshift cells to either side of them. Alice pushed open the door to her right. "Erin said that when someone had been purchased they were moved into the main house to be prepared for the delivery."

Alice could tell Joshua's reaction mirrored hers by the way he ground his back teeth.

"How long would that process take?" he finally asked.

"She wasn't sure because she'd only heard rumors. She guessed it could take anywhere from a couple of days to a few weeks. They got to shower daily, eat better and were taught how to dress and wear makeup." The last word came out with disgust.

"What if they rejected the help?" Joshua asked.

"Then they were punished in front of the other girls to make sure the next one complied." She pointed at the corner where a water hose snaked around a bale of hay. "Some were stripped and then blasted with water."

"That water would be freezing this time of year," he ground out.

Alice nodded. "If that didn't work, they were beaten."

Something very dark passed behind Joshua's eyes and he didn't immediately speak. "I'm guessing the stubborn ones were used for the baby farms."

"They'd keep a couple on hand, locked inside the house." Alice wasn't sure she could handle seeing what was inside there being a mother herself but she would force herself to if it meant finding Isabel.

"No drugs for impregnated ones because that would damage the babies," he deduced.

Alice nodded. That's what Erin had said.

"This is the stall Erin said she was in with Isabel," Alice said, standing in front of the second stall to the right.

"You want me to check it for you?" Joshua asked.

Alice shook her head as she stepped inside the open door. "Come with me?"

He nodded and followed her inside.

She dropped to all fours, skimming the ground, moving pieces of hay out of the way.

"What are we looking for?" he asked.

"I know Erin has good intentions and I don't think she would lie," Alice started.

"But she'd been drugged and we can't exactly rely on her information to be accurate," he finished.

"I need something more, some evidence she was here in the first place." She touched the half-heart pendant hanging from a silver chain around her neck. "Isabel always wore the other half to this."

"I wondered about that," he said.

"Erin didn't remember seeing it but Isabel never took it off." Neither did Alice.

"It could've been hidden under her shirt," Joshua said.

"I was thinking the same thing." Alice's hand ran over a small object in the corner. She brushed hay out of the way to get a closer look, praying it was the other half to her necklace. No such luck. She tossed the small stick aside. Just as she started to tell Joshua to look for the chain, commotion from behind stopped her.

"You shouldn't be here alone," Fischer's voice boomed.

Joshua was already to his feet, blocking Fischer's view of Alice. "She isn't."

"Last I checked, neither of you had authority to investigate this case," Fischer said.

"Then it's a good thing you're here," Joshua shot back, unmoved. The man was steel under pressure.

"You wanted to talk to me about Erin?" Alice asked, redirecting the conversation as she stepped beside Joshua. The thought of all those scared girls huddling in their corners filled her with new resolve. At least this group would be home for the holidays with their families. Yes, broken and damaged, but alive. The healing could begin. It wasn't exactly a great situation for anyone involved, make no mistake about it, but it was a start and more than Isabel had.

Fischer nodded and then led them out of the barn to a shaded area under an oak tree with a picnic table underneath. She noticed that he stood rather than sit and then propped his left foot on the bench. That was no subtle reminder that he was the one in a position of authority. She'd been attracted to his arrogance when they'd first met, confusing it for confidence. Maybe having the boys had changed her because she much preferred Joshua's quiet strength.

Alice shivered as the frigid air cut through her light jacket. Joshua, cool as ever, seemed unfazed by the weather and especially by Fischer as he leaned against the oak's thick trunk, arms folded. The two men couldn't be more opposite. Fischer was territorial and quick to anger whereas the calm cowboy kept a level head under all conditions.

She'd wondered what she'd say to Fischer when she saw him again. As it turned out, she felt sorry for him. He was the one missing out on the two greatest boys in the world. It was his loss.

"Erin said the girls were given a glass of water and told to drink it all so they could sleep on the first night. She doesn't remember much after that, so it was obviously laced with some kind of drug. I'm guessing ketamine because she felt aware of what was happening to her but she couldn't move," Alice said.

"Could've been GHB or Rohypnol. Did she say if the water tasted different? Salty?" Fischer's lips thinned and his tone was clipped.

Alice was already shaking her head. "She couldn't tell a difference. Said that she felt like she was in a dream and she had trouble remembering even simple things. Her arms and legs felt numb and she remembered the odd feeling that she couldn't control her body. When she woke the next morning all her personal belongings including the clothes off her back were gone and she was given jeans that were too big and a baggy T-shirt to wear. She had makeup on that she had never worn before and was thrown into the shower and told to clean herself up. She overheard a few of the men talking and realized that first night she was photographed."

"So, either Perez has the pictures sent directly to his clients or there will be a website," Joshua said, a spark of hope in his voice.

"I've got tech guys working on it right now," Fischer said. "I know you're hoping to find information about Isabel."

"Yes."

"We'll do everything we can to locate her," Fischer said and she hated how perfunctory it sounded. She wasn't a random civilian who had no idea the odds of finding Isabel at this point. Yes, the probability increased exponentially having both her and Joshua on the case. Fischer most likely would throw extra resources in the mix, too. And none of that guaranteed a good outcome.

Alice pushed aside her despair in order to fill Fischer in on the rest of the details as evidence was carefully removed from the scene. With any luck, the tech gurus would unearth information that would put all the pieces of the operation together and then arrest warrants could be issued. In a worst case, they wouldn't get anything more than they already had. Fingerprints from the trailer were a good start. A good prosecutor could work with that if they could find Perez.

It's more than we had yesterday. She would grip that thought with both hands.

"Who do you have back at the sheriff's office interviewing the men who were picked up?" Alice finally asked Fischer.

"I'll be talking to them myself. Right now, I'm sweating them a little bit. Giving them a chance to think about how little their boss actually cares for them now that they've been arrested. I've already planted the seed that the girls are talking and that the guys should've been more careful around them. Then, I gave implicit instructions to my team to leave both of them alone until I return. I want to oversee every aspect of the interrogation," he said. It was just like Fischer to want to control every detail. He planned everything to a T. Her pregnancy was one of the curveballs he couldn't handle but in this case she was relieved. He would be thorough.

"Thank you," she said quietly. "Will you ask about Isabel?"

"Yes," he said.

"What else can I do?" she asked, trying not to sound as helpless as she felt.

Fischer took a step closer to her and lowered his voice. "You could go out to dinner with me."

"Not a good idea," she said a little more emphatically than she'd planned.

"You're welcome to hang out at the sheriff's office where we're setting up camp. The sheriff has also arranged for us to take over a house nearby. We plan to stick around in town until we see this through."

"I want access to the house," she said, nodding toward the small ranch-style on the property.

"As soon as my men finish processing it," Fischer said, glancing at his watch. "Give me a couple more hours."

Alice didn't want to think about the evidence that might be bagged up—evidence that might lead her to Isabel—walking out of there. She needed a quiet place to think this through. The cold was starting to get to her and she tried not to think about how little the girls were given to keep warm in that barn.

"I can drive you wherever you want to go," Fischer said.

"Thanks for the offer, but—"

"Are you ready?" Joshua asked Alice, stepping away from the tree.

Fischer shot him a look that could freeze alcohol.

"Yes," she said to Joshua. Even with the few

good hours of sleep last night, she could feel her bones ache for more.

An agent wearing cargo pants and a dark jacket jogged over to Fischer before she had a chance to get up. "Sir."

Fischer introduced him as Special Agent Lund.

"We found that item we discussed," Lund said, holding out an evidence bag with his gloved hand.

Fischer put on a pair of latexes and reached into the bag, pulling out the other half of Alice's necklace.

"That belongs to Isabel." Alice produced hers.

"I know," Fischer said. "I read about it in the file."

Tears stung the backs of her eyes as she processed what seeing the necklace meant. Isabel had been here. She'd been in that house.

And now she was gone.

"WHEN YOU SAID you owned a ranch, I thought you meant like a couple of acres and a one-story house with a barn in back," Alice said, staring at the grand colonial two-story with black shutters bracketing the windows, grateful for the distraction from churning over the same dark thoughts about what might've happened—might still be happening—to Isabel. Alice needed to stay positive and there wasn't much else she could do until Fischer let her know it was safe to go inside the ranch at the compound. She refocused on the house in front of her, trying to lift her mood. This place oozed holiday and family and love. Equally grand were the white columns adorned with thick strings of holly. Christmas-red ribbon twined throughout the greenery. Despite her heavy mood she couldn't help but feel the spirit of the holiday looking at the house and wonder how much her boys' faces would light up seeing a place like this. "Those French doors are gorgeous."

Joshua smiled.

From each window—and Alice counted fourteen including the French doors—a massive wreath hung complete with a red bow on top and a candle in the center. The porch stretched easily to match the width of the house, although *house* seemed like such a small word for this grand place. Large pots of holly with red ornaments flanked the couple of stairs to the veranda where pairs of white rocking chairs were grouped together on both sides.

"Do you own this place?" she asked, feeling suddenly out of her element. The amount of time she'd known the cowboy could be reduced to days but in her heart she felt like she'd known him so much longer. So, this was a shock. This was another side to him that she had no idea. Besides, he acted nothing like the kind of wealthy man he'd have to be to own this place. Once again, he shattered all her preconceived notions about Texas cowboys.

"A piece of it," he said and he sounded a little awkward about it. "My brothers own the rest."

"I'm sorry. Is that a sensitive subject?" she asked as he parked, remembering that his parents had died.

"Not really," he said and then shrugged. Not exactly convincing.

"I feel like you know everything there is to know about me, so I'm not going inside until you bring me up to date on you," she said, not making a move to unbuckle.

"There's not much to tell," he said.

She rolled her eyes.

"Okay, my parents grew a successful cattle ranch. Dad built the business from scratch, slowly buying the land around us. Then, he started a rifleman's club and, together, my parents made more money than they could give us or spend, so my mother threw herself into charity work."

"They sound like good people," Alice said.

"They were."

"I'm really sorry for your loss," she said, and meant it. Sitting in front of the house they'd built, on their land, she felt an unexplainable connection to them.

"Thank you."

"I can tell that you loved them very much. So, forgive me for asking but why did you go into law enforcement? Don't you like it here?"

"I love this land," he said so defensively that it almost sounded like he was trying to convince himself, too.

"I wasn't trying to question your devotion to your family," she said, wishing she had better words to express herself.

"This is where I grew up and it holds a lot of great memories. I love my brothers and being close to them is the biggest bonus to being here," he stared.

"But—"

"I never signed on in life to be a rancher. This path was chosen for me and I've always been expected to take my rightful place beside my family. I figured that I'd come to terms with that someday or convince my parents otherwise but then suddenly everything changed when they died and it felt selfish to chase my own dreams. So, I've done what was necessary to fulfil my role. I figured that I would *want* to at some point in my life after I'd gotten other things out of my system. I just never expected to come back this soon," he said and she appreciated his honesty.

Alice touched his arm, ignoring the electricity pulsing through her fingertips, wishing a few words of comfort would come to mind. They didn't.

"So, you gave up your job and moved back here?" she asked.

"Sort of. I'm on leave. My parents had homes built for each of their sons at various spots on the land. My place is on the northwest side of the property, next to Diamondhead Lake." He took the key out of the ignition, unbuckled his seatbelt and opened the driver's side door.

Alice met him in front of the Jeep.

"I miss being on the job. It's part of who I am. So I understand what you're saying." Alice fell in step beside him. "Who lives here now?"

"A wing was opened up years ago for club guests and there are offices on the other side. Janis lives in the main house."

A stab of jealousy shot through Alice. "Janis?"

"She worked with the family for years before my brothers and I voted to give her a share of the property. She's like family," he said, stopping at the front door.

"That was kind."

"It was the right thing to do," he said.

"You always do the right thing?" she teased, trying to infuse a little humor to break up the otherwise heavy mood.

Joshua turned to face her, wrapped his arms around her waist and pulled her flush against his body. His lips were so close to hers, she could breathe in the scent of coffee. "No."

He closed those intense green eyes. And then he kissed her.

Chapter Twelve

Kissing Alice wasn't in the plan. Then again, most of Joshua's ideas about his life had been turned upside down in recent months. Why should this be any different?

Pulling on all of his strength, he took a step back. She felt a little too right in his arms, fit him a little too well and he wasn't sure what to do with that.

"Are you attracted to me?" she asked, lips full and pink. He tried not to stare at them.

"Without a doubt."

"Then what's the problem?" she asked with a flush to her cheeks that nearly did him in.

"If the timing was different," he started but she waved him off.

"Don't say it. I know," she said. She was beautiful, no question. There was so much more that attracted him. She was smart and funny. He wasn't much of a talker but conversation with her came easy and he actually liked it. There was something about the way her curves fit him when he held her while they slept. And for all her exterior toughness, he could see just how vulnerable she was inside—that was especially the part that drew him in. She was determined and could be a little reckless but only with herself. She was careful to protect people she loved and anyone she believed to be innocent.

Alice was pretty much everything that had been missing in the women he'd dated up to now. But she needed to be off-limits. As soon as the FBI called for an interview, he'd be gone and she needed someone who could stick around in her life. Be there for her and her boys. A stable force for Isabel. Besides, the father of her twins had just walked back into her life. There was no stronger bond than family and he had to give Fischer a fair chance at winning her back.

So that kiss pretty much went against everything Joshua believed in. And yet he still couldn't help himself. No matter how powerful a pull his attraction to Alice Green became, Joshua needed to "man up" and be stronger. For her sake and that of her family. He'd never forgive himself for getting in the way of a family. Plus, he had nothing to give to her. His own situation was a mystery and he'd be gone the second the feds offered a job. If that didn't happen, he needed time to reconcile his life. To make his brothers understand that he wasn't abandoning their parents by choosing a different path. *Whoa.* Was that really how he felt?

If he was being honest? Yes.

What could he give her if he felt trapped in his own situation?

Against his better judgment, Joshua twined their fingers together and led Alice into the house.

Overanalyzing the kiss was a big mistake. It only led to more questions with no easy answers.

"The inside of this place is even more beautiful than the outside, if that's even possible," Alice said, motioning toward the dual staircase and he tried not to focus on how much he liked the sound of her voice. Or how right it felt for her to be there in his family home.

For the time being, he wanted to take her mind off her problems and get some food in her so she could keep up her strength. He tried to tell himself that was the only reason he'd opened up to her about his personal circumstance and not because of his growing feelings for her or that part of him wanted her to know the real him before she walked out of his life.

"Now that's a table," she said, blue eyes wide, as they walked into the kitchen. "I bet you could seat fifteen people if you needed to."

"Janis always teases us that we have no manners but the truth is we all like eating in here better than the formal dining area. Always have. I guess we figured that room was meant for holidays and guests," he said with a chuckle.

"What is he accusing me of now?" Janis rushed in, wearing her full holiday gear.

"Being a great cook," Alice said quickly. "My boys would love being at a place like this. The decorations are beyond amazing."

Janis was short, little more than five feet and she had those grandmotherly soft features and a figure that could best be described as round.

Joshua introduced the two of them with a half smile. "Janis goes all out this time of year through New Year's. She keeps this place running and has been helping my family most of my life. Would you care for some cider?"

"Forgive the outfit." Janis motioned toward her black pants, white shirt and red apron. Her head of white hair had been fixed in a loose bun. She could be a dead ringer for Mrs. Claus in that getup.

"I think it looks fantastic," Alice said and her face lit up. "It would be a huge hit with my boys."

"Where are they?" She looked around.

"I'm from Tucson. They're home with a sitter while I investigate a missing teenager," Alice said.

"Must be hard to be away from them this time of year," Janis said and then embraced Alice in one of her warm hugs.

Joshua had squirmed out of that grip more than once as a teen, reluctant to show just how much he'd needed it at the time. He blamed teen hormones and all that came with them. He gave the two women a private moment while he scooped out two cups of cider that was mulling on the six-burner.

By the time he set them on the wood table, Alice and Janis joined him.

"The Nelson widow really outdid herself this year," Janis said.

Joshua almost laughed out loud. "Does she normally wear her red silk robe to greet guests?"

"I was talking about the bronze," Janis said on a laugh, shaking her head. "That must've been a strange sight."

An emotion crossed Alice's features that looked a lot like jealousy. She had no idea.

"Awkward is a better word," Joshua said.

"I'm sure it was. A woman her age." Janis made a tsk-tsk noise.

"How old is the Nelson widow?" Alice asked.

"She must be going on seventy by now," Janis responded.

Alice's tense expression broke into a wide smile. And then she laughed. The sound filled the air and brightened everything it touched.

"Sure, it's funny to you," he quipped. And then he laughed, too.

"I better change out of these old clothes," Janis said on that note, turning to Alice. "It was nice meeting you."

"She's a wonderful person," Alice said when Janis disappeared down the hall.

"Yeah? Don't let her hear you say that. She'll never be able to walk through the door again for how big her head'll get," he teased, enjoying a relaxed moment with Alice. There was so much trouble brewing around them, he liked being her temporary shelter.

"I heard that," Janis quipped from the hallway.

"Good. That's why I said it so loud," Joshua said with a wink toward Alice.

Her smile was better than a string of a thousand sparkling lights. He'd given himself another problem because his thoughts kept rounding back to that kiss.

After warming up with a hearty bowl of vegetable soup, Alice's expression turned serious.

"I feel like I'm so close to breaking this case open but answers are just out of reach." She absently fingered the half-heart necklace. "Now that I know Isabel was there, I hope I can find something to give me a direction at the ranch house."

"Sometimes, it helps to think about something else for a little while," he said, glancing up at the wall clock after hearing the whop-whop-whop of chopper blades. Good. His delivery would be right on time.

"I probably shouldn't ask this but I hear a helicopter outside. Does it belong to you?" Alice asked.

"It's my brother's but we all use it when needed."

She leaned back in her seat as the text he'd been waiting for arrived. He palmed his cell and sent back their location in the kitchen.

"This is crazy. I mean, you don't seem like a rich man and I thought all ranches struggled to make ends meet," she said.

"Some of the smaller ranches have been affected by the economy but we've been fortunate over the years. This is a large place. We sell beef from longhorn, breed them with Hereford and sell that, and then there's the Rifleman's Club, although our members call it the Cattlemen Crime Club because they like to sit around and discuss crimes. I'd like to show you the property sometime." One of the things Joshua loved—loved? Maybe appreciated was more the right word—about Alice was her strength. Her determination was a close second. Being in law enforcement suited her and that was fine. But when she came home, she deserved a place like this, a place he knew she'd be safe where she wasn't constantly putting herself in harm's way. Maybe the package he was about to deliver would make her think twice before she jumped into another dangerous situation.

"I'm sure your brothers need you around here and I've been taking up all your time," she said. "If you want to drop me off at the station I can catch rides with some of the guys."

"You asked me about law enforcement work before and I never really answered. The truth is that I do miss it. So, stop trying to kick me off the team," he said, revealing another truth about himself he hadn't planned on.

The conversation was about to change dramatically, he thought, as the back door opened and Ryder burst through.

"Everything okay?" Alice said with one look at him.

He was healing fine and that's not what she

was talking about. It was the distraught look on his face.

"Not really," he admitted with a laugh. "I just spent two hours in a helicopter with a pair of twins. I don't know how in the hell our parents survived our childhoods."

An older woman walked in with a twin on each hip.

For the second time, Alice's face lit up. "How on earth did you get here?"

A chorus of "Mama!" followed the twins' entry.

Their bodies started twisting and turning as she hurried to them. Joshua noticed that she winced as she took them, so he moved to her side and helped get her to a chair. She sat, one on each knee, and must've kissed each of them a good twenty times. Her smile, that amazing smile lighting her face, was the best he'd ever seen.

The pint-size boys were the spitting image of their mother, both blonds but their hair was short and curly. Joshua could see their blue eyes from across the kitchen when they first came through the door on their babysitter's hip. Darn cute kids.

"Hedi-copter," one of the twins said, babbling in a language only his brother could understand.

"Was that fun?" Alice asked with the biggest smile Joshua had seen on her face yet. And there was something right about him being the one who put it there.

INTRODUCTIONS HAD BEEN made and the twins were finally settled for a nap in one of the guest rooms on the ground floor. Marla decided to rest with them, saying she could use a few minutes of downtime after the exciting helicopter ride.

Alice couldn't remember the last time she'd been this happy. The boys loved crawling around the house and being outside in the backyard, and she enjoyed every minute of playing with them. She strolled into the kitchen as relaxed and happy as she could be under the circumstances.

"Thank you," she said to Joshua. "How on earth did you arrange this?"

"I thought you could use a morale boost," he said, offering a cup of coffee. "And I have my ways."

"People say that laughter is the best medicine," she said, taking the warm mug. "But I'd say those people must not have kids because one kiss from those pudgy faces and my mood is up here." She held her free hand as high above her head as she could reach.

"Good. I'm glad my plan worked without repercussion. I wondered if you'd chew me out for putting your boys in a helicopter with my brother at the gears," he teased.

"Are you kidding? I missed them too much to care how they got here. As long as they made it safely, you won't hear a complaint from me," she said, taking a sip and enjoying the liquid as it warmed her throat. "Fair warning. I don't think I'll be able to convince them to leave without taking Denali home with us." She referred to the family's Labrador retriever.

"He's a good sport and especially loves children. I don't think he's played that hard or licked so many faces since he was a pup," Joshua said.

The twelve-year-old chocolate Lab had let her boys follow him around and laid still while they climbed all over him and tugged at his ears. Alice had been quick to make sure they didn't do anything to hurt Denali.

"He's beautiful," she said. "Fits in perfectly with this place, which is filled with—" she was at a loss for the right word so she settled on "—magic."

"It's a good place," he agreed and there was an emotion behind his eyes that she couldn't quite put her finger on. "I have a family meeting to attend in about an hour. Want to go for that walk I promised you now?"

With Marla settled in with the boys Alice didn't have to worry about hovering over them. Plus, this place had better security than Fort Knox.

"Why not." She emptied her mug and set it on the counter, energized from the caffeine, sure, but mostly from seeing her boys, hugging them. There really was something magic about baby hugs.

Joshua stopped at the door and offered his arm. She took it and he ushered her out the door and into the crisp late afternoon air. The sun was shining, warming everything it touched.

"Which direction is your house?" she asked as they walked to the white wooden fence around the yard.

"That way." He pointed northwest. "I'll take you there sometime."

"How about right now? Is it far?" She glanced at the house where her boys were sleeping. She'd been content to watch them sleep but didn't want to take a chance of disturbing them. Her two energy-fueled boys needed their rest and she didn't even want to think about the consequences of them not getting it.

"It's too far to walk. We'd have to grab a golf cart."

"Maybe we should wait until the twins wake.

I don't want to miss a second of them with their eyes open."

"They're great boys," he said.

"For all my jokes about never sleeping and never sitting down since they were born I wouldn't change a thing, except maybe to make them grow up a little slower," she said. "Find a 'pause' button somewhere."

"Time speeds by," he agreed. "Even without having little guys around to remind you just how fast."

"And it can change just like that." She snapped her fingers.

Joshua's gaze dropped and his jaw clenched. She was referring to Isabel's kidnapping but she'd struck a nerve with him. He had his own investigation going on. "Are you really okay?"

"Yeah, sure." She didn't want to give away her emotions, emotions that left her feeling overwhelmed and running on empty. Seeing her boys and being with Joshua were the only two positive things in her life right now.

"A lot has gone on in the past few days. It's a lot to process."

"I'm one of these people who's calm in the moment and then it hits later." When she was alone in bed. How many nights had she cried herself to sleep in her lifetime? More than she cared to count or admit.

"I know you like to play tough guy and you put on a good show. Do people who really know you believe it?" he asked.

"Yeah, they have to. My job and my life depend on it. I don't have to tell you how important it is for fellow officers to trust that you can do your job," she said, wishing she could let down her guard a little more.

"You don't have to be like that with me," he said, his voice a low rumble. "I'm not a threat."

She couldn't let his words affect her, so she took a step back to put some distance between them. "That's where you're wrong."

Joshua gazed out onto the expansive property looking like he was letting her words sink in.

Alice needed to change the subject because that conversation wasn't going to lead where she wanted it to go and should know better than to want.

"You said before that your parents were murdered. Do you want me to take a look at the file and give my professional opinion?" she offered, wishing there was something she could do to repay him for everything he'd done for her. "Sometimes it helps to have a second set of eyes."

Before Joshua could answer, the sound of

gravel crunching underneath tires caught both of their attention. A brand new dual-cab Ford F-150 pulled down the lane.

"That's my Uncle Ezra," Joshua said as he checked his watch. "He's early."

Alice watched Joshua walked away, thinking that she wasn't the only one who'd mastered the tough-guy routine.

"I WOULDN'T HAVE called this meeting if it wasn't important," Uncle Ezra began and Joshua wondered if there'd ever been a time when Ezra didn't think that what he had to say was worthy of everyone's immediate attention.

His brother Tyler was the best negotiator, so he sat to Ezra's left at their father's conference table. Ezra had been given the right-hand seat to their father, his chair now empty and a constant reminder of the loss the brothers felt, as a gesture but he wasn't given any real responsibility. To the right of Tyler were Uncle Ezra and Aunt Bea's spots. The next empty seat, directly opposite of Dad's at the long oak conference table, belonged to their mother. To her left were Janis, Ryder, Colin, Joshua, Austin and Dallas. Dallas's seat was directly opposite Uncle Ezra.

"We need to address—"

Dallas put up his hand to stop Uncle Ezra. "Not everyone's here yet."

Uncle Ezra stood in a huff. "Who else is invited?"

"We can't have an official family meeting without everyone present, Uncle Ezra. We're still waiting on Aunt Bea," Tyler, ever the calm negotiator, said.

"But I specifically asked for a meeting with the brothers only," Uncle Ezra complained, his hands planted on the oak table.

"That's against policy and you know it. You wouldn't like it if someone tried to exclude you from important family business," Tyler continued.

"Which is why I'll never understand why she's here." He motioned toward Janis as she picked imaginary lint off her sleeve with a here-he-goes-again look on her face.

"Everyone's clear on your vote to keep Janis out of the family's interests. The rest of us disagreed and majority vote ruled," Tyler continued. "Can we put this discussion to rest or do we need to readdress bylaws every time we meet?"

Uncle Ezra blew out a puff of air and then moved to the coffee tray set up near the door.

Ryder leaned toward Joshua. "For someone

whose vote literally counts for nothing in our business this guy sure calls a lot of meetings."

"And he sure is full of a lot of hot air," Janis whispered, leaning toward them both.

Joshua and his twin brother smirked.

"Well, I'm glad *he* decided to join the meeting this time," Uncle Ezra said. His gaze locked on to Joshua.

Before Joshua could respond, Aunt Bea rushed in.

"Apologies to keep everyone waiting," she said in her best sugary-sweet voice. Joshua wasn't sure whether she spoke like that just to get on Uncle Ezra's nerves or if she was being true to herself. The two matched about as well as a rose petal and a cactus, both personalities multiplied in the presence of one another. That's not where their differences ended. Where Uncle Ezra was thin and wiry, Aunt Bea made up for it in girth. Despite her hearty size she was inclined toward floral dresses and matching hats with ribbons, and she always dressed like she was on her way to Sunday service. The brother and sister had a long history of being at odds that ran deeper than their physical appearances.

"It's kind of you to finally show, Bea," Uncle Ezra countered, ever the gentleman.

"Let's get to business," Dallas said. Even

though all brothers had equal share of the ranch, they'd voted Dallas in charge due to his natural leadership tendencies and the fact that he was willing to take on the job no one else wanted. "You requested this meeting, Uncle Ezra. What would you like to discuss?"

"Since my brother passed, God rest his soul, I think the burden of running this place has been a lot to put on you boys as you straighten up your affairs," Uncle Ezra said.

"You've said that before and we appreciate your willingness to help," Dallas said.

Aunt Bea made a disgruntled noise.

"As I've said before the division of the family business—"

"Of our father's business you mean?" Joshua couldn't help himself. Uncle Ezra was always trying to make it seem like he'd contributed to the success of the ranch and club even though he hadn't lifted a finger.

Uncle Ezra shot him a look that almost made him laugh out loud.

"At least some of us are willing to pitch in during times of crisis," Uncle Ezra continued, another dig toward Joshua.

Instead of responding, Joshua leaned back in his chair. His phone buzzed in his pocket. He fished it out, didn't recognize the number. He excused himself and took the call in the hallway.

"Mr. O'Brien, this is Rupert Grinnell with the personnel department of the Federal Bureau of Investigation," the male voice said.

"This is an honor, sir. I've been looking forward to this call," Joshua said, hoping this meant what he thought it did, an interview.

"We're impressed with your background, Mr. O'Brien. We'd like to bring you in to talk to a few people," Grinnell continued.

"I'd like that very much," Joshua said.

"Are you available in two days for an interview?" Grinnell asked.

"Yes, sir," Joshua said with a pang of guilt that he might be walking away from Alice when she needed him. His brain kicked into high gear. He'd be gone a day at best. He could leave early and might even be able to make it home in time for dinner. They were getting close to blowing the Perez case wide open and surely they'd find something concrete on the computer that would help them locate Isabel. They were in a holding pattern for now anyway.

"My admin will contact you with the details," Grinnell said. "I should tell you that there haven't been a lot of applicants we've been this interested in for a while."

"I appreciate the confidence, sir. I look forward to the meeting," Joshua responded.

He ended the call and then reclaimed his seat in the conference room. He should feel elated and yet he couldn't deny feeling like he was sneaking around, doing something wrong. He chalked it up to abandoning his brothers and the fact that he felt like he was letting his father down in some way, feelings he'd felt his entire life.

The next time his phone buzzed, it was a message from Tommy. The crime scene was clear and he and Alice were free to examine it themselves.

"Which brings me to my dilemma." Uncle Ezra didn't miss a beat. Joshua would have to ask Ryder if he missed anything important in the last few minutes. Somehow, he doubted he had. "I'd like to do more. Given the recent… *news*…about your parents I'm sure you'll want to put all your extra resources into helping solve the investigation." Making a play for more power while their heads were still spinning about the fact that their parents had been murdered was right up there with one of the slimiest things he'd ever proposed.

"I'm not saying that any of us agree to this, but I'm guessing you have something specific in mind," Dallas said and Joshua knew his brother was digging around to find Ezra's real motivation behind the proposal.

"Given that I'm always willing to pitch in when needed whereas Bea is content to collect a check, I feel that it's only fair that I receive a larger piece of the responsibility." He should've said what he really meant...a larger piece of the *pie*.

This wasn't his first play for more so no one freaked out but Bea did make that grunting noise again.

"As you know, we can't give more to you without taking away from others," Dallas said, impatience edging his tone. "And Dad's instructions were pretty clear as to how he wanted the place divided. If he'd wanted you to have more, he'd have given it to you."

"It's not necessary to be so formal," Uncle Ezra hedged. "We can deal with the legalese later. I'm talking about something temporary and unofficial here. I've had my lawyer draw up papers so everyone's on the same page." Uncle Ezra opened the folder he'd brought with him and pulled out what looked like a contract.

"For a document that isn't supposed to be official, he sure went to a lot of trouble," Joshua whispered to Ryder, who lifted an eyebrow and smirked.

"All of those in favor of considering this request, raise your hand," Dallas said, obviously getting impatient with this conversation.

No hands went up, save for Ezra's.

"All against," Dallas said, his hand was the first to jut into the air. "Motion declined. This meeting is—"

"Now, just a minute," Uncle Ezra interrupted. "You didn't hear me out."

"I think we're clear on where you stand. So I'll be clear on where we do. Making demands isn't going to get you where you think you should be. Neither is trying to slip a legally binding document under the radar. So, back off or we'll exercise our legal right to have you removed from this company." Their father had given them a way out. All they had to do was unanimously vote to remove Uncle Ezra. No one would go against Dad's wishes, though, unless his brother got out of control.

"That would be a long and costly process," Uncle Ezra said.

"I sure hope that wasn't a threat," Dallas countered.

Uncle Ezra's phone buzzed. He was probably looking for a distraction when he answered the call. He turned his back to the group and lowered his voice enough that Joshua couldn't hear what he said. Uncle Ezra ended the call a few seconds later. When he turned around, he looked a little pale.

"Who was that?" Dallas asked.

"The Johnson boy," Uncle Ezra supplied, quickly regaining his disgruntled demeanor.

"What does Tommy want?" Dallas asked the question on the tip of everyone's tongue.

Uncle Ezra stuffed the pages inside the folder and tucked it under his arm. "I'm sure it's nothing. Said he wants me to come down to the station to answer a few routine questions to help him out with my brother's case."

"I HOPE THIS doesn't become a theme between us," Joshua said to Uncle Ezra, following him outside after the meeting. He'd scanned the kitchen for Alice, figured she was somewhere with her boys when he didn't see her.

"What's that supposed to mean?" Uncle Ezra seemed committed to playing dumb. His uncle looked a little more rattled than usual.

"The jabs back there." Joshua wasn't one to mince words.

Uncle Ezra whirled around just before reaching his truck. "You and the others are blind to what's going on around you. I see this situation for what it is." He thumped his chest and his voice was sounding a little hysterical.

"Easy there, Uncle Ezra. You don't need to have a heart attack," Joshua said.

"It wouldn't surprise me if I did," was all Uncle Ezra said back. He turned, opened the door to his truck and then slammed it after climbing inside the cab.

What was that supposed to mean?

"Think he's going to give us a problem?" Joshua asked Dallas as he returned to the kitchen and told him about their exchange.

"Yeah, he'll be a pain in our backside for the rest of his life," Dallas quipped.

"About what he said earlier about me, I know—"

"No need to worry about what that old coot thinks," Dallas said. "We all have previous business to take care of before we can fully devote to the ranch. That's why we work together to ease the load."

Joshua wanted to tell his brother that he had no plans to stick around if the FBI offered him a job. He'd pretty much decided that he wouldn't anyway. There were other branches of law enforcement that he could work for and his former chief had placed him on temporary leave rather than process his paperwork, reminding him how tough it could be to get back into law enforcement once he left voluntarily.

Keeping the secret was eating at him. Telling his brothers was the only fair thing to do.

What if he didn't get the job at the FBI? He could always change his mind and decide to stay at the ranch. After all, nothing was out of the question and there was a big part of him that started feeling at home there recently. Maybe he could settle into a role?

Alice walked into the kitchen with a baby on her hip and froze. He could tell by her reaction that she was overwhelmed by all the O'Briens in one place. He crossed the room to her and she relaxed the minute she made eye contact with him.

"Alex is hungry," she said.

"What do you need me to get?" Joshua was ready to roll up his sleeves. He also needed to tell her that she could have access to the whole crime scene now.

"Marla said she left the formula and bottles in the diaper bag under the table." She scanned the room.

Everyone kept right on talking as if she wasn't there, a fact she seemed to appreciate. They were used to strangers being in the main house. Janis was there, too, and she seemed to know on instinct what Alice needed, bringing over the bag.

"I'm happy to help make a bottle," she offered.

"That would be great actually," Alice said trying to hold the baby and navigate the contents of the bag. She looked happy, really happy. Joshua didn't want it to end and he knew it would as soon as he told her.

"You want me to take him?" Joshua offered, unsure of how to hold a baby or toddler, whatever this little guy was. He held his arms out and the little boy leaned toward him. Joshua took that as a good sign. "Come here, buddy."

Surprisingly, Alex didn't scream. Joshua bounced up and down anyway for good measure.

"Who have you got there?" Dallas asked, turning his attention toward the little boy. His brother had had a crash course in parenting after meeting and falling in love with a single mother. He and Kate were now proud parents of a little boy by the name of Jackson who she'd adopted before meeting Dallas. He had already declared his intention to officially become Jackson's father after the wedding. Joshua may not have been around the ranch as much as he felt he should be, but he'd been around enough to witness the changes in his older brother, the happiness and peace having a family of his own brought.

"This is Alex," Joshua said, and then introduced Alice. He'd barely noticed that the room had gone silent and everyone's attention shifted to Alice and the baby. "There's another one just like him in the other room named Andrew."

"Twins?" Dallas asked as their brothers took turns welcoming the newcomers.

Joshua nodded.

"I'm not touching that one." Dallas's hands came up in the surrender position.

In that moment, in that room, Joshua felt like he belonged right where he was.

"Bottle's ready," Janis announced. "Can I do the honors?"

Alice smiled and said, "Yes."

Which was probably a good thing because Marla walked in a few seconds later with Andrew and Alice had to get busy making another bottle. Once Marla was settled with Andrew, feeding his bottle, Joshua handed Alice a fresh cup of coffee.

Everyone sat at the table together for the first time in weeks. And also for the first time, Joshua felt like he was right where he was supposed to be. A moment like this was rare and like snow on the ground in Texas, it wouldn't last. He'd get restless and need to get back on the job.

Speaking of which, he turned to Alice. "We're clear to examine the crime scene."

Chapter Thirteen

The air was cold, the sky a foreboding shade of gray. Alice shivered to stave off the chill.

"Tommy hasn't shared any information from the crime scene with you, has he?" she asked Joshua as they pulled up.

"They've picked up a lot of prints and other DNA evidence," he said, which could tell them which rooms Isabel had been in. Alice already knew she'd been there based on the necklace find.

"Hopefully, they'll be able to link these crimes to Perez," she said, holding on to the thought that all wasn't lost. Bad men had been taken off the streets. Eighteen girls had been rescued and were beginning a journey toward healing.

"Since they tried to torch the trailer, he's checking the database to see if he can get a hit on similar crimes in the Southwest," Joshua said.

"Maybe they'll find other locations," she said. It was a smart move and something she would've done in order to learn everything about the man she was pursuing. The more she knew, the easier it would be to anticipate his movements. Perez was still out there, somewhere. She scanned the cul-de-sac as she exited the Jeep. And he knew where Isabel was.

The sun hid behind the clouds, lights were out inside the ranch-style house, giving it an eerie quality.

Alice pulled her jacket closed tightly in an attempt to keep the biting wind from penetrating as she ducked under crime scene tape and crossed the yard. It was day five of her burn and her nerve endings were waking up. Her forearm hurt and she refused to take anything stronger than an ibuprofen, needing a clear head.

The lack of activity, the quiet, was a stark contrast to her earlier visit. Walking inside the house made chills run up her spine. She'd been to dozens of crime scenes in her career and this one was right up there with the worst of them. Places like this had their own feel, as if the horrors carried out there imprinted the air, the walls. It was as though terror and desperation had a physical manifestation that couldn't be cleared out by opening the windows and airing the place out.

Alice stepped inside the too dark living room. Neither she nor Joshua would open the curtains. Both would tread lightly at the scene on the off chance investigators needed to return. The room had an old brown plaid sofa, something that looked left over from the seventies, off to one side. There was a card table and chairs. All the laptops had been confiscated, the data being pored over by technical experts.

The place had a filthy half frat, half junkyard feel. Stacks of newspapers were on the floor and the center of the table. She shuffled into the kitchen where there was a coffee maker and a microwave. Dirty dishes filled the sink along with a few cigarette butts and there were a couple of flies buzzing around the empty pizza boxes on top of the counter. The place looked and smelled like it hadn't been cleaned in months. She doubted it had ever truly been scrubbed. She had an urge to throw on plastic gloves, grab a bucket and some soapy water and scour the place clean. The dirt could be wiped off; those were temporary marks. Her urge had so much more to do with what lay beneath the surface, what a bucket of soap and water couldn't erase.

"Looks like the team swept the place pretty well," Joshua said. He was taking the scene in for himself and Alice could feel his eyes watching her for a reaction, maybe a breakdown. He stood beside her in the otherwise empty room.

The tremors started slowly and from a place deep inside her. Thoughts of Isabel in this horrible scene assaulted her. These were exactly the kinds of weaknesses she'd suppress if she stood there with anyone else. But this was Joshua. He was so tall, so muscled, and yet all of his strength came from within, like he had a bottomless well to draw on.

Alice turned to face him. He didn't seem to need her to spell it out. He just held her. His arms circled her waist as she buried her face in his chest. She didn't know if the holidays had her feeling vulnerable or the fact that this crime scene hit her right at home, but she needed him in a way she'd never allowed herself to need anyone.

The scene they'd walked into was something out of a horror show and her personal connection to it had her rattled to the core. And yet, standing there with Joshua, his arms around her, leaning into his towering strength, Alice finally knew what it was to feel safe. Isabel had had her family. She'd gone to sleep with this feeling every night. And Alice needed to return that feeling to Isabel.

The ranch had three bedrooms and no basement thanks to the shifty clay soil in Texas. It was a similar deal in Arizona. Using her phone's flashlight, Alice walked into each room. All were similar, a bed with a tether, blankets scattered on the floor and those damn buckets that had probably been taken outside and rinsed out once a day. There were cosmetics in the bathrooms and bindings in the showers so that the girls could be tied up and left alone. A few nice outfits hung in the closet of the master. The others had been boarded up. There was very little in the way of furniture. Pillows, blankets and towels scattered across the filthy gray carpet. Alice wouldn't let an animal live there, let alone a young girl. Another wave of gratitude hit her at the thought of eighteen girls going home. There was so much heat on Perez he wouldn't strike again anytime soon. For the moment, his operation was on lockdown. That fact brought another wave of thankfulness.

Alice studied the beds, the walls of each room. Inside the bedroom farthest from the main living quarters, she dropped to her knees beside the bed and searched for any clues. Beside some of the beds were notches in the floorboards. What did they mean? The obvious answer was a girl marking the days she spent in that room. There were other scratches, too. At least one was a set of initials. The marks in the last bedroom were different from the other two. Instead of straight up and down marks like ticks, they had more of a pattern. Alice snapped a picture so she could study it later. Her phone buzzed in her hand, startling her.

"I need to see you," Fischer said before she had a chance to utter a greeting.

"What is it, Fischer?" she asked, the urgency in his tone not exactly a welcomed sign.

"In person or no deal," he practically grunted. More of his manipulation tactics. Well, no thanks.

"Tell me on the phone or not at all," she said, not willing to play games.

A sharp sigh issued through the line.

"There was only one set of prints on the necklace and they belong to your friend," he finally said. At least he'd cut to the chase.

"She was here. I had no doubt it belonged to her." No one had stripped the necklace from Isabel and that was the first positive thought. So, had Isabel taken off the piece of jewelry in hopes that Alice would find it? She'd be smart enough to realize leaving a trail would help Alice find her. *Keep hoping, sweetie.*

"This isn't the right time but I need to talk to you about our boys," Fischer said.

"Okay." She'd received confirmation that she was on the right track in looking for Isabel. She was close. For the first time in a long time she felt a very real sense of hope, like this might not end with her finding a body. Everything else could be recovered from. Alice was living proof. She glanced up at Joshua. He was a comforting presence. And for the first time, she saw a future.

"When?" Fischer asked.

"Now."

"Like right now?" he asked.

"There's never going to be a good time for me to talk to you," she said. "So, tell me what's on your mind."

"I should see them," he said low into the phone.

"That's probably a good idea." She'd be more enthusiastic if Fischer hadn't used the one word that made it seem like he was only asking out of obligation...*should*. More confirmation that she and Fischer would never be on the same page in life. His job would always be more important, would always come first. Alice was career minded. She understood devotion to the job. This was something different. It was more like hiding from real life in a career.

"You didn't cash the checks," he said.

"No." She didn't owe him an explanation.

"I've been saving the money anyway," he said. "Didn't feel right about keeping it."

"How about I let you put them through college?" she asked, letting him off the hook from the day-to-day.

"Deal." There was a lot of relief in that one word. "Alice. Be careful with this investigation. I'm doing everything I can to help you but there's only so much I can do and my superior is pushing me to arrest you."

She ended the call, stood and asked Joshua to take her home.

JOSHUA OPENED THE door to his place—a place he'd basically avoided moving into save for his bed—and navigated through stacked boxes to his kitchen. All the basics were there for making coffee. He ate most of his meals on the go or at the main house. And he noticed how embarrassingly little he had in the way of real supplies. Up to now, a microwave and a basic plate would've covered all his needs. He wished he'd done a better job of making the place presentable now that Alice was there.

His house could best be described as a rustic log house. It had four bedrooms, which he'd protested at the time it was built, only one of which was furnished. Before meeting Alice, four had seemed like overkill. Now, he wished he'd furnished them all so she and the kids could stay over instead of at the main house.

Furniture was sparse. There was a sofa in the middle of the living room. He'd positioned it to take advantage of the fireplace. There were a few bar chairs huddled under the granite island. His mother had spared no expense with the finishes and Joshua suspected she'd done that to entice him to move home sooner.

Now that Joshua really thought about it, his apartment in Denver had had a similar unfinished feel, barely any furniture and not enough kitchen supplies to cook up a decent meal. He'd worked evenings and ate out most meals. He'd kept a decent coffee maker, and a guest room with a bed in case one of his brothers came through town.

"I love this place," Alice said as she took in the tall beamed ceilings in the living room.

"I'd like to say that I had a hand in building it but that would be a lie. My mother oversaw all the details," he admitted.

"It fits your personality to a T," she said, walking into the kitchen, eyeing the chestnut cabinets and stainless steel appliances. She smoothed her hand across the island. "And this granite is just…perfect."

"Thank you." It shouldn't matter so much that a stranger liked the place. "You want a cup of coffee?"

She nodded as she settled into a seat at the island. He could see in her expression there was a lot rolling around in her mind.

"It might be helpful to go over what we already know," he said, handing her a fresh cup, ignoring the thought that having her at his place made it feel more like home. He chalked it up to this year being odd without his parents and that was true enough but there was so much more he didn't want to analyze. His life had other complications. He still hadn't figured out how he was going to tell his brothers about the call he'd received from the FBI that afternoon asking him to come in for an interview.

It's just an interview, he told himself like there would be any discussion if they offered a job. He had every intention of taking it on the spot. He'd wanted to be with the FBI since he was old enough to know what the letters stood for. Even so, he felt like a liar for not telling his brothers. *Or Alice*, a voice reminded.

Alice took a sip of the fresh brew. "I keep thinking where she could be and come up empty."

"What about the picture you took at the

crime scene? Any thoughts pop into your mind as to what those marks are about?" he asked.

"They aren't consistent with the ones in the other rooms and that makes me think they're significant. Or maybe hope's the right word." She shrugged. "Fischer said Isabel's necklace was found in the same room."

Otherwise, the trail to Isabel had gone cold and Alice was becoming discouraged.

"How about the piece of jewelry?" he asked.

"The necklace didn't have any prints other than hers, so that leads me to believe she was the one who took it off. I have to think that was on purpose, especially since the necklace is intact."

"Agreed," Joshua said, taking a seat next to her at the counter.

"Which leaves us with the fact that we know she was there but we have no idea what happened to her next." There was so much pain in Alice's eyes, so much tension outlined in the brackets around her mouth. "I'm not sure I like this part better."

"It might take the tech guys a few days to figure out what's going on, but they're the best and I have every hope they'll find what we need," he said.

"And that should be reassuring except that there could be unimaginable horrors happening to her right now and I can't stop it." Alice's shoulders deflated as despair sank heavy.

Joshua gripped his mug.

"I know I shouldn't obsess over it and I should stay positive, but how can I not?" she asked, frustration rising. "This is the closest I've been to her in weeks and I can feel it in my bones. I'm missing something and if I can put that final piece together, I can find her."

"Everything that can be done is happening right now," Joshua said in an effort to soothe her. His words seemed to have the opposite effect.

Alice smacked her flat palm on the granite. "If that were true, she'd be home right now."

ALICE KNEW FOR certain that if she were a better detective Isabel would be safe right now. There was nothing the cowboy could say to convince her otherwise. "I know you're trying to be helpful but I have to face facts."

"And those are?" He folded his arms and leaned against the counter.

"Being here isn't helping find Isabel," she said flatly. The reality was that she couldn't get too comfortable, not while Isabel was still out there missing. "I appreciate everything you've done for me. Being with my boys brought me back from a dark place and I'm grateful for that."

"But?"

"You've done everything you can and the rest is up to me. You've helped me get this far but my arm is improving and I need to get out there on my own."

"If he gets to you, it's game over," Joshua said. "You know that, right?"

"I can't care about that right now." That wasn't entirely true. Alice twisted her hands together. She had two boys in the main house who desperately needed her. It wasn't like there was a father around. She was all they had, for better or worse.

"Then what about Alex and Andrew? Stay here for them," Joshua said.

"And what? Be the kind of mother who can't look herself in the mirror?" She took a deep breath to ease her tension. Didn't work. "That's exactly how it will be if I don't find her."

"I get that," he said, his voice calm. And that probably angered her even more. He was too calm when she wanted to scream.

"No, you don't. You've never caused a child to lose both of her parents and then be pushed into the foster care system," she said a little too loudly.

"I'm sorry," he said quietly.

"Words can't take away the pain," she fired at him, anger building inside her like an out-of-control storm. Talking about the past wasn't something she'd ever done with anyone, not even the sheriff and his wife. They'd accepted her for who she was and taken her in, showed her kindness. But they'd never forced her to speak of the horrors she'd experienced. Now that she was older she realized there had to have been a file on her somewhere and she was certain that both the sheriff and his wife had read it. Maybe that's why they hadn't forced her to speak about her past.

"No, they can't and I won't pretend to understand what you've gone through," he said in that infuriatingly calm voice of his.

"People have been through worse," she said because that was the only mantra she knew. The one that had gotten her through several beatings and two attempted sexual assaults before the age of fifteen. Foster care could be great. She'd seen it work with the sheriff and his wife. And it could be the worst possible hell. She'd seen that side, too.

"Worse than what?" he pushed. "Being locked in a closet?"

"Those were good days at some places," she said, anger a rising tide inside her.

"Being hit?" His calm voice barely breaking over the whoosh-sound thrashing in her ears.

"You're getting closer," she said. "Try being

whipped with a cord but only in places that can't be seen so you wouldn't have to miss school the next day."

"I'm sorry." His words were quiet but he'd broken the seal on that topic.

"And then there was the time my 'uncle' Ralph forced himself on top of me while I was trying to do homework on my bed." Her pace picked up. "I stabbed him with my pencil and he beat me to within an inch of my life."

"I'm so sorry." Those calm words broke through the anguish in her mind.

"Or how about the time I dropped the bowl of mashed potatoes on Thanksgiving so I was forced to pick my switch from the tree outside and then I was beaten before being locked in my room with no food." She couldn't stop now that those floodgates had been opened.

"You shouldn't have had to go through that," the calm voice said.

JOSHUA DIDN'T LIKE pushing her but there was so much she was keeping inside, burying. He knew exactly what that could do to a person. He'd lied to both his parents, said everything was fine when they were laying out their grand plans for the future, plans that he'd agreed to even though everything inside his body said no. He'd sat at the same conference table he had earlier with his family and let his future be laid out for him. And now he couldn't take any of it back.

"People go through worse. Every single day," she shot back. "There's nothing special about me."

"There's where you're wrong," he countered.

"I'm not." She stopped in front of him, her glare daring him to argue. Her shoulders were tensed, her hands flexing and releasing and there was panic in her eyes. Maybe she was afraid to feel special.

"Do you ever do anything to make yourself happy?" he asked.

"What's that supposed to mean?"

"It's a simple question. I'll rephrase it. When was the last time you did something for yourself?" he asked.

"Why is that important?"

"Because it's important for me to know," he said as calmly as he could. The truth was that with her so close his heart was thumping in his chest. It was taking pretty much all the willpower he had to stand there, a foot apart, without touching her. There was anger in her eyes but there was something else, too. Trust.

"To be honest, I don't really think about myself much."

"Do you think other people are like that?

That every person looks out for others in the way that you do?"

"I don't know." She shrugged. "I guess not."

"You know they don't. You've seen it first-hand. You've been bounced around, mostly to places that were a living hell. I'm amazed that you dedicated your life to upholding the law because one look at the statistics says you should be on the wrong side." He'd seen enough of that side through the charity work his mother was involved in and the stats were downright depressing. Most kids brought up in an unstable environment ended up unstable adults. It was like bad seed planting bad seed, perpetuating itself all over again.

There was fire to her eyes now. Fire and spark. It was what he'd come to love about her. Hold on...

Love?

That was a strong word to describe his feelings.

"I had a choice just like everyone else. Bad things happen to good people all the time and whatever happens in childhood isn't a child's fault," Alice said and he already knew he was in trouble with her. "But the day I turned eighteen I figured that I had a choice about my life. I could blame my rough situation on everyone else and be miserable. Or I could take charge of my life and find happiness. Not that I'm all that great about that last part. I make mistakes, but I'm giving my best effort."

Alice stood toe-to-toe with him now. What she lacked in height she made up for in spirit.

"You didn't answer my question," he said. Staring into those blue eyes was like looking straight into the sun. He was going to get burned. He just didn't know to what degree.

"I didn't want to but I'll tell you what scares me," she said.

"Okay," he said, arms folded, feet positioned in an athletic stance.

"I'm scared to death that I'll mess up my kids. Or worse, they'll end up in the system because their father didn't want anything to do with them and I land myself in jail because I do something stupid," she said.

"You're doing better than you think," Joshua said. "Your boys are amazing, happy."

"Rambunctious," she added and he had to smile.

"I wouldn't have it any other way." It was true enough. The pair of them were lively. But they were also like a sunny day after months of cold, hard winter. "You won't go to jail. I'll see to that."

"And what if you're not around?" she asked.

It was a good point.

"Where am I going?" he asked. He had every intention of making sure she was okay.

"There are two times when I'm truly happy," she said and her words came out like a dare.

"Okay." He readied himself for pretty much anything.

"One is when I'm with my twins and we have the whole day together with nothing to do but hang out and play," she said and her entire demeanor softened.

"And the other?" he asked.

"Right now. When I'm with you."

Chapter Fourteen

Joshua knew that he was going to pay for this later, but he hauled Alice against his chest anyway. Her scent, fresh flowers and clean, filled his senses. He'd memorize that scent for when she disappeared into her own life in Tucson and he spent lonely hours on the job. A flash of his apartment in Denver invaded his thoughts. There'd been very little furniture, only the necessities for day-to-day living. There'd been months on end of cold, gray skies. Looking back, it seemed so…empty.

Instead of wallowing in that thought, he buried his face in her hair. Her hands were on either side of his face now and she was guiding him to her lips.

They'd need to take it easy and that was going against everything inside Joshua's body. Strung taut, his muscles vibrated with tension that begged for release. He would have to take it slow, careful. Counter every primal urge inside him because he wanted to go fast and hard and lose himself inside her.

When their lips touched, electricity hummed inside his body searching for an outlet.

His arms were already around her waist as he bent down and scooped her up, her legs wrapping around his midsection. His erection was already painfully stiff, pressing against the denim of his jeans, and he'd never wanted a woman like he wanted Alice. Her skin was soft, silky against his.

"Take me to bed," she said and his feet were already moving, their breath quickening. His heart was a hammer against his rib cage.

"I don't want to hurt you." He eased her down on the floor at the foot of the bed.

She grabbed the hem of her shirt and pulled it over her head. He watched for any signs of pain that movement caused and was relieved when there were none. Any indication and he'd force himself to stop, somehow.

"You can't," she said with a look in her eyes that said he couldn't physically hurt her anyway. Emotionally, well, he didn't even want to go there. He was already in too deep.

Joshua had another problem. He needed to slow their frantic pace or this whole thing would be over before it had a chance to get good. He smirked. "You're beautiful, Alice."

"No, I'm not." She blushed, her cheeks flush in the light from outside his window.

He ran his finger along her lacy bra before unsnapping it in the front. She shrugged out of it and her full breasts felt silky and hot against his palm. Her nipple beaded and he groaned. "Then you don't see what I see."

Her hands were already tugging at his shirt, so he discarded it on the floor next to her pile of clothes. His jeans and boxers followed a half second later and he stood there, naked, just as she was. Her body shone in the moonlight and it was about the sexiest thing he'd ever set eyes on.

He started with her shoulder and kissed her, tenderly. He moved down to the stab wound on her side and feathered a kiss above the bandaging. Moving slowly, his lips grazed her ribs until he could easily access her bare breast.

Alice mumbled something he didn't pick up with a little moan as he took her nipple in his mouth.

And then his lips trailed down across her firm belly. His movements were fluid, careful. The next second, she was on the bed, positioned at the edge, her legs apart.

He pulled a condom from his bedside table

and fumbled as he rolled it over the tip of his erection, hands shaky with need...a need for Alice. And then he was inside her, her hands around his midsection, urging, as he drove deeper.

The sound of pleasure that tore from her throat egged him on. He pulled back and then thrust again. She joined his movements, slow and precise at first, that built to a frantic pace as both struggled to breathe, needing release.

Her muscles tensed and her breath held, so he drove faster and harder until she shattered around him. A single thrust and he detonated inside her in an explosion that rocked his core.

For a long moment, neither moved, frozen in time, neither wanting it to end.

Until they repositioned onto his bed, under the covers, their arms and legs tangled, warm bodies together in the chilly evening.

Joshua held on until he could feel her even breathing, her sweet sounds of sleep.

And then he let go, too, full of the knowledge that he was in serious trouble with her in his arms.

THE NEXT MORNING, Joshua stretched, untangled his limbs and then forced himself out of bed to make coffee. He could lie there all day with Alice, her warm smooth skin pressed to his.

Okay, he'd better cut it out before he created a problem that couldn't be fixed while she was sleeping. He finished his first cup and opened email on his laptop. His itinerary was there. He'd leave tomorrow morning on an early o'clock flight. He needed a ride to the airport.

Ryder would be up since it was already light outside so Joshua called his brother's cell.

"Did you hear about the meeting tomorrow morning?" Ryder asked. "Eight a.m."

"No." Joshua scanned emails until he found one from Dallas. He quickly read it. "What does Uncle Ezra want now?"

"Same thing as always, I guess. Our land," Ryder said.

Joshua had no interest in fighting the same battle over and over again. It was already time to let go and move on.

"I need a favor," he hedged.

"Okay."

"I need a lift to Houston Hobby early tomorrow morning."

"Where are you headed?" Ryder asked.

"Just some business I need to take care of." Joshua tried to sound casual.

"We have that meeting," Ryder said.

"You'll be back in time to make it. I'll call in from the airport," he said, felling another bite of guilt because they both knew he wouldn't.

"Where are you headed?" Ryder asked, leaving it alone. Joshua was grateful.

"Up north. Have to talk to someone there. I'll be back tomorrow night and I'm hoping to get another ride," he said, giving his brother the details. "You can fill me in on the Uncle Ezra situation."

"Sounds like a plan," Ryder said and Joshua was pretty sure he picked up on a hint of disappointment in his brother's voice.

He hated feeling like he was letting his family down.

"Thanks, bro. See you tomorrow morning," he said. He moved to pour his second cup of coffee as Alice entered the kitchen.

"What was that all about?" she asked and he wondered how much she'd heard.

"I have a meeting tomorrow out of town. It'll be an in-and-out trip." It wasn't a lie and yet it sure burned like one. Joshua moved to her, kissed her. She looked amazing wearing the flannel shirt he'd left out for her. "How about a cup of coffee?"

She didn't immediately respond, just bit her lower lip and then nodded.

Joshua poured two cups and handed one over.

"I can't stop thinking about those marks." She picked up her cell phone and located the picture she'd taken last night of the floorboard at the compound. She set the phone down in between them, studying it while she sipped her coffee.

Joshua was grateful for the change in subject. He didn't want to lie to her, *couldn't* lie to her. And yet he wasn't ready to tell her, either. He was stuck in a weird space not knowing what he really wanted. Ask him yesterday morning or the days leading up to it and he would've answered that he wanted that job more than anything else. Last night had changed things. Now, with her in his house, he wasn't so sure. He'd go to the interview and see how he felt after. He'd know one way or the other once the job was offered, *if* the job was offered.

The rest of the morning was quiet. He picked up breakfast from the main house after seeing her twins off with Marla back to Tucson. Joshua had another one of those weird feelings in his chest, a stir from somewhere deep, as he buckled them into their seats on the helicopter.

Alice spent the balance of the morning online trying to figure out what the scratches in the picture meant—I III II B \/ I-I—and came up empty.

Joshua had had a few food supplies delivered so he fixed sandwiches for lunch and made her promise to rest on the couch. Curled up with his laptop, she looked right at home there. And a very big part of him was ready to claim her as his. But then there was something else on Joshua's mind. Something that had been eating away at the back of his mind and he needed to talk to her about it because he was falling down a rabbit hole with his emotions and he needed to know if this, whatever *this* was, was a good idea.

"When you were talking about Fischer the other day, you said he's 'technically' the father of your twins." Joshua paused for a beat. "What does 'technically' mean? He either is or he isn't."

"The only tie he has to my boys is shared DNA," she responded and her voice was even, indicating no deception.

"That is the substance that binds a person together," he countered. "It's what makes families and that's powerful if you ask me. Not something that can be shoved aside or ignored."

"True. If he wants a relationship with the boys, I would never stand in his way. They have a right to know their father as much as he has a right to know them. As for anything between the two of us, well, that possibility died when he walked out two weeks before they were delivered. I gave it a chance before and nothing has changed since. We spoke the other day and I let him off the hook with helping care for the boys. He sounded more relieved than anything else."

"It's pretty clear that the man still has feelings for you," Joshua said.

"Yeah, well, me and my boys are a packaged deal," she said quickly. "As for Fischer and me, I'm done."

Joshua took a sip of his coffee. He wanted to think over what she was saying. He couldn't imagine not knowing his own sons. First of all, the twins were pretty darn cute. They had personalities to match. What if Fischer spent time with them and decided he wanted to play Dad? Would it be right for Joshua to stand in the way of a family?

Knowing how important sharing the O'Brien name with his brothers meant to him, she would easily be able to understand why he'd see this issue more as blank and white. But then, she had to have figured out that no O'Brien would walk away from his own child.

"Besides, there are stronger and more important forces in the world than shared genes," she said after a thoughtful pause and he realized that she'd been staring at him the whole time.

"Yeah, like what?" Joshua asked.

"Love."

Chapter Fifteen

By the time Alice woke the next morning, Joshua was gone. The bed felt too big without him and she lay there an extra few minutes breathing in his unique masculine scent—clean and spicy—that lingered on the pillow and sheets.

Alice threw the covers off and her feet over the side of the bed keenly aware of the fact that it was Friday. She stretched, amazed at how fast her burn was healing. Her stab wound was better, too. She'd have to remember to send Dr. McConnell flowers when this whole ordeal was all said and done. Alice shuffled her feet into the kitchen and then made a fresh pot of coffee. It was her second favorite scent, next to Joshua's. Speaking of which, he'd said that he'd call once he landed in…wherever he'd said he was going. Or did he?

She probably forgot. Her mind had been pre-occupied with the case.

After a few glorious sips of coffee, she phoned Marla to check on the boys. Her sitter didn't have anything new to report except how excited they'd been at riding in the helicopter again. Marla admitted to being thrilled about that fact herself.

After hearing an earful of baby talk, Alice ended the call and refocused on Isabel, desperately needing to redirect her attention or risk crumbling into a ball for how much she missed her family.

Alice had considered every angle she could think of for the marks. There was something familiar about the pattern but she couldn't figure it out. Could it spell out a name? It was a stretch and a fairly long one. Isabel would be smart enough to make it difficult for the men in the next room to be able to tell what she was doing and that could account for the fact that the markings were different. Alice spent a good two hours skimming every document that came up with no luck. Her stomach growled, convincing her to get up so she could eat.

Isabel's birthday loomed. The boys' birthdays were early into the New Year. No way did Alice want to make it through the holidays without Isabel home. *Where are you?*

Glancing around Joshua's place, she noticed that he didn't have a tree or much of anything else for that matter be it Christmas or otherwise. Pretty typical of a man's house, she thought. Except for the fact that there were unopened boxes stacked in almost every room. She thought he'd said that he came back there to live but another thought struck. Was he planning to stick around? From the looks of the place the answer to that question was no.

JOSHUA SHOULD BE the happiest guy in the world, he thought as he unlocked the door to his home. The house was dark, which meant Alice was already asleep. It was good to be back. He stepped inside and punched his security code into the pad near the back door. He rearmed the alarm before quietly setting down the paper he'd carried with him. The interview had gone well. Better than well. He'd been offered his dream job—a job that would be waiting after a few more steps in the process. So, why did he tell the director he needed time to think it over?

On the trip home, he'd told himself that he wanted to run it by his brothers before he accepted. He didn't want to acknowledge the real reason was that he wanted to talk it over with Alice. His feelings confused the hell out of him but nothing in his world felt right without her.

After a shower, he slid under the covers and Alice, still asleep, rolled over and curled around him. There were other problems stewing in the back of his mind. Isabel was first and foremost and then there was trouble brewing between Aunt Bea and Uncle Ezra. According to Ryder, the two of them were fighting worse than usual. Joshua chalked it up to the fact that his father had been the one to keep things settled between them. Ezra was making moves to push her out, but then he wanted Janis out as well. The two of them were known for fighting but was something else going on between them besides sibling rivalry?

Aunt Bea was getting flustered and the boys were quick to jump to her defense. Everyone dismissed Ezra as harmless, saying he was a sentimental old fool. But was he?

He'd been using his ranch money to finance other projects, unsuccessful ones. But that wasn't the most disturbing news. Dad would roll in his grave if he knew that Uncle Ezra was involved with the McCabe family, their father's rival.

After the meeting, they'd resolved to keep Uncle Ezra in check and start digging around in his personal affairs to make sure he wasn't in over his head somewhere.

Joshua tossed and turned, unable to give over

to sleep. Was it really family business keeping him awake or was it something more? His guilty conscience?

All he needed was a few hours of sleep to get through a day. He checked the clock as his phone buzzed.

"I shouldn't be making this call," Tommy whispered and he sounded anguished.

"What is it?" Joshua shot up. Alice was already up and hopping into a pair of jeans that had been laid out on the dresser.

"Perez has been seen in town. The informant said to watch out for a white van. He's on a mission and Fischer thinks he's back to take you down. He's sending someone your way to intercept Perez. Keep your guard up," Tommy said. "I have to get back in my office so the task force can see me. They've been keeping close watch on my every move."

"Do you have a general vicinity for Perez?" Joshua asked, already half-dressed.

"He's outside the city limits, heading east." A shuffling noise came through the line before Tommy ended the call. He was smart enough to handle his end, so Joshua wouldn't worry about that.

"What did he say?" Alice asked, already buttoning up her shirt.

"Perez is here." From the time of the call to

sitting in the Jeep was less than a minute-and-a-half. He could fill her in on the road.

"THE HEAT IS ON. Looks like Perez is making a run for me. I'm guessing that also means he's cashing out his interests in this area and about to disappear for a while," Joshua said to Alice as soon as they were on the two-lane highway outside the ranch.

He cursed.

"What is it?" she asked.

"I need gas," he said.

Alice's thoughts raced. Perez could not get away. A cold chill trickled down her spine. She didn't want to hope that Isabel could be with him because that would be too much of a coincidence and, frankly, Alice wouldn't be that lucky. He could give answers, though. He would know where she'd been sold. She could force him to talk. He was finally within reach and she couldn't allow this chance to slip through her fingers.

"There's a shotgun tucked behind your seat," Joshua said, eyes on the road, pedal to the metal. "My Glock's in the glove box. Which one do you want?"

"I'll take the shotgun," she said, figuring she could get a wider spray that way in case she had to give chase. "But I need Perez alive."

"I know we do." Joshua's focus stayed on the patch of road ahead. He slowed as he approached a gas station and then turned in.

At the second pump, there was a white van.

"He's here." She expected him to say they should call it in and wait. The man at the pump was pushing on the van, shaking it, holding the dispenser in his hand while trying to squeeze out that last little bit of air in the tank. Another few seconds and it would be too late.

Joshua pulled in front of the van, blocking it, like he was getting in line for the pump. His headlights would keep the driver from getting a good visual on them.

Pump Man glanced around, caught on to what was going on, and fiddled with the lever on the dispenser. Alice realized the guy was engaging the lock mechanism that would keep gas pumping before he tossed it toward the Jeep and then hopped into the van. The engine hummed and he must've put the gear shift in Reverse. Gravel spewed toward them as the van peeled out and then spun backward.

Joshua ran toward it, took aim and nailed the front tire. The van turned so hard it tilted to one side and Alice was half afraid it would roll over. She had no idea who might be in the back or how many people but she knew in her heart that innocent girls were in there.

She ran into the stretch of highway that would put her directly into the line of the van.

All it would take would be one shot, she thought, as the van's headlights stared her down.

The driver could gun it, and he might do just that, so she spread her feet in an athletic stance and took aim, her finger hovering over the trigger mechanism.

If she went down, she was taking the driver with her.

The shell was engaged in the chamber and she was good to go. She could get off a shot and, hopefully, roll out of the way into the ditch before the van hit her. Unlike in Hollywood movies, a man who'd been hit didn't immediately drop. There was only one shot capable of instant death and it was nearly impossible to pull off even for a trained sniper. That was a bullet straight to the brain stem.

No way were her boys becoming orphans.

Alice was a decent marksman, especially for a cop. But she wasn't *that* good. Almost no one was. And she didn't exactly feel lucky. Besides, if she believed in luck she figured she'd used all hers to get to this point.

No, the kind of shot she could get off was different. With a direct hit, it would take a while for Pump Man's brain to catch up with the news that he was hit, and essentially already dead. He'd keep on doing whatever it was he'd been doing before the shot had been fired. In this case, that meant he'd floor the pedal while locked on to her. Buckshot would spread and Alice could end up killing innocent girls in the back of the van.

Staring at the white van, she realized what seemed so familiar about the markings in the picture… Isabel was giving her a license plate number. Roman numerals I, III, II, so 132. And then the others B \/ I-I, BVH. The license plate was 132 BVH.

The engine revved, threatening her. This whole scene had been reduced to a game of chicken.

If her plan worked she'd be safe. Her boys would have a mother. Alice thought about that as the van kicked toward her. It took a few seconds for the wheels to grab the blacktop.

Alice couldn't risk killing anyone else inside the van, so she jumped toward the ditch and rolled, came up with the shotgun so she could shoot the driver at closer range as he blew past.

As it turned out, she didn't have to. The cowboy took a shot from the gas station side of the street and pegged the driver, who wasn't Perez. He never saw it coming because he was too busy looking at Alice with his foot on the brake.

There was no one in the passenger seat. If Perez was inside that van, he was in the back.

Alice darted around the side of the vehicle just as Perez rounded it. The shotgun barrel was too long and it was too easy for Perez to knock it out of her hands. He was strong, aided by adrenaline. He swung his right fist, connecting with her left cheekbone. Alice's head shot right and she felt warm liquid in her mouth—blood.

His elbow came up to her throat and he slammed her into the van. She coughed, her lungs clawing for oxygen.

No way was he getting away. Not this time.

Perez was stronger than her, no doubt at it. Trying to overpower him physically would be a mistake and possibly cost her life. Alice dropped to the ground and swept her left foot, catching his legs as he attempted to flee. She twisted her legs around his ankles in a scissor-like grip and then rolled like an alligator. He bit the dirt hard, trying to wrangle his way out of her grasp.

Too bad, jerk.

She folded forward, reared her fist back and then fired a punch, connecting with his stomach before he knocked her out of the way. She threw another punch, determined to inflict as much pain as she could and hopefully wear him out enough to cuff him. This scumbag was going to jail.

Just as he managed to wriggle away, she caught the butt of the shotgun with her hand. She gripped it with both hands and then pumped the handle. And then a thought dawned on her. Shoot him and Isabel could be lost forever.

Perez spat in her direction, those snakelike eyes bearing down on her. Chicken. He was daring her to shoot.

And then, Joshua whirled around the van and tackled Perez.

Alice pushed up to her feet in a swift motion, shotgun in hand. Joshua had Perez on the ground in front of her. She fired off a kick, connecting with Perez's thigh as he writhed on the ground underneath the bigger man's heft. She tossed the shotgun aside and pulled zip cuffs from her hip pocket.

Joshua shifted position enough to allow her access. She jammed her knee into Perez's back and hauled his arms behind his back. He spat and cursed as she zip cuffed him. When the dust settled, he was going to have a nasty headache. And he was going to spend the rest of his life in jail.

"I'll be right back," Joshua said and she knew he'd be securing the driver and checking for additional threat inside the van.

"Where is she?" Alice asked, forcing Perez onto his knees.

"You think I'm telling you, bitch?" Perez spat.

Alice walked around to face him, needing to look into his eyes. Then she remembered the license plate number and she knew in her heart that she would find Isabel. "You don't need to."

"I have three girls in the back of the van," Joshua shouted.

There was a faint wail of sirens in the distance. She picked up the shotgun and aimed the barrel at a spot on Perez's forehead. "Give me a reason to shoot."

THE SUN WAS rising and the forecast said the cold front would break later that morning. Warmer weather was on its way.

Fischer had run the license and produced an address. The address belonged to a middle-aged dentist.

Perez and his men were in the minivan in front of Joshua's Jeep as they blazed toward the home of the dentist across town.

"We're bringing her home today," Joshua said quietly, his gaze focused on the road ahead.

She wanted to believe those five words so badly her heart ached.

"I sent Ryder for the boys," he added.

"There are no words to thank you for everything you've done for me," Alice said and she meant it.

"She'll want to see them and your family deserves to be together." He turned right behind the minivan.

The street was quiet and in the part of town with expansive front yards and large two-story houses. Disgust rippled through Alice as she thought about the horrors going on behind the doors of at least one perfect-looking house with a manicured lawn.

"I need to tell you something," he said.

"Okay."

"I've been offered a job at the FBI."

"Is that why you went out of town? To interview?" she asked.

"Yes."

"Why didn't you tell me before?" she asked, trying to block the hurt that came with him keeping a secret.

"Before I met you that was my dream job. Now, I'm not so sure." Red brake lights illuminated in front of them as the minivan stopped in front of a huge house with white siding and black shutters. There was a large concrete porch. Everything looked so peaceful, so suburban.

Men exited the minivan and circled the

house as Alice jumped out of the passenger seat of Joshua's Jeep. She barely heard him say something about them talking later over the sound of her hammering heart. For one, Joshua could be leaving soon for a new job. Her heart didn't even want to go there. And then there was the obvious anxiety that came with a bust.

The dentist was about to go down.

Fischer stopped Alice before she walked onto the property.

"Let me go in," she pleaded.

"I'm not here to stop you. I'm here to thank you," he said.

She bit back her shock. "Okay."

"I mean it," Fischer said. "The devotion you have toward this girl who you obviously love tells me that you're an amazing mother to the boys."

"Thank you," she said, noticing he hadn't said *our* boys. And it was just as well. Her heart belonged to another man anyway.

"If you ever need anything, you know where to find me. Now it's my job to warn you to stay back," he said and then turned toward the house.

She understood what he was really saying. He couldn't technically allow her to be part of what was about to go down but he could look the other way.

Alice stalked around the porch, trying to get a view of the layout of the house. Joshua was right behind her, his calming presence keeping her from losing it. This was it. Isabel was here. And she was taking her home. Only where was that now? Her heart said with Joshua.

Bam. Bam. Bam. The sound of an agent banging on the front door echoed in the crisp morning air. The sun warmed her back as she heard the door open.

A man cried out as agents stormed the place, pushing past him, searching for Isabel. One of the men stayed back to deal with the dentist.

Alice was supposed to wait, but she couldn't. With Joshua's steadying force behind her, she flew toward the front door.

The dentist was already on his knees, his hands clasped on top of his head, and it took everything inside Alice not to hurt him the way he hurt others. He looked like someone she'd see at the library browsing, not a child molester. But then, experience had taught her that there was no type.

"I never meant to hurt her," he repeated over and over again as he must've realized his life was going to be spent behind bars.

Isabel might be in one of the bedrooms and all those would most likely be upstairs, so Alice darted toward the staircase. As she ran up the first stair, she saw her and froze. Isabel looked frightened and weak next to the agent helping her at the top of the stairs. But when she spotted Alice, her face changed.

They met in the middle of the stairwell and embraced.

"You're safe now," Alice said, tears streaming down her face as she held Isabel in her arms.

"I knew you'd find me," Isabel said softly, crying.

"You're coming home."

With those words, the teen sobbed.

Joshua wanted everything to be perfect for Alice, Isabel and the boys. He called ahead to the ranch and made arrangements for everyone to stay there a few days while waiting outside the hospital room.

Isabel needed to be examined by a doctor for forensic evidence purposes and there was a counselor on hand to begin the process of guiding her toward recovering from the horrible ordeal she'd endured. She was strong and that girl deserved to have the world at her fingertips. He would do everything in his power to ensure she got it.

Then there was Alice. Also strong and so tough on the exterior with such heart and tenderness on the inside. He'd never met a woman like her before and his heart said he never would again. Which was why he was determined to keep her in his life one way or the other.

The flurry of activity in her room had slowed and a nurse finally exited, saying she was ready to leave.

He stepped inside Isabel's room. She was smiling through tears and talking quietly with Alice, who had introduced them earlier.

"Are you ladies ready to go home?" he asked, and he meant his home—a home he wanted to share with them.

"Yes," Alice said as Isabel nodded.

THE STEAKS ON the grill smelled amazing. It was Sunday supper at the O'Brien ranch and the whole clan had turned out to send Alice and the kids off as they prepared to go back to Tucson the next morning.

Fingerprints and DNA found at the ranch matched Perez and his men and all were facing spending the rest of their lives in jail.

Joshua had spent the past week getting to know Isabel and he'd developed fatherly instincts he didn't know had existed before. He'd finally taken the time to unpack boxes at his place on the ranch and Alice and Isabel seemed to enjoy decorating together. Even Denali had made fast friends with Isabel, but then she really was a sweet teenager.

He glanced across the lawn and his heart was full. Tommy was there and he'd offered Alice a job if she ever wanted to come back to Bluff.

Alice had practically forced Joshua to take the job at the FBI and he'd be heading to Quantico for twenty weeks of training next week.

And yet, his heart knew he would never set foot on that plane.

He located Alice, who was standing next to his favorite tree and made a beeline toward her. She glanced up, saw him coming and her smile eased some of his overwrought nerves.

Taking her in his arms, he whispered three words he'd been needing say all morning, "I love you."

There was a pause before Alice said, "I love you, Joshua O'Brien."

That was all he needed to hear.

"I don't know how I'll survive being so far away," she said.

"Then, don't leave."

She pulled back and examined his face. It seemed like she was checking to see if she could believe her ears. "I want to stay. But it's complicated with the kids."

"It doesn't have to be." He bent down on one

knee and produced a little red box from his pocket. He opened it and the diamond sparkled as though he'd captured Christmas in a box. "If you'll have me, Alice Green, I'd like to marry you."

She looked directly into his eyes. "No one has ever made me feel the way you do. I can't imagine loving anyone more but—"

"Don't say anything else until you hear me out."

She nodded.

"I love you, Alice. I've never felt this way before about another person. I love our boys and Isabel, this ranch. You and the kids are what have been missing here for me. And I want to spend the rest of our lives together, on this land, bringing up our children. There's a lot to figure out but we have all the time we need. Will you do me the honor of being my wife?"

She kissed him and they both glanced over at Isabel who was already nodding her head. The half-heart necklace she wore sparkled in the sunlight, made whole by the one around Alice's neck.

Alice turned back to Joshua. "With everything in my heart, yes. You, this place, have felt like home from day one. I can't wait to make a life together here."

The rest of his brothers crowded around, celebration in the air.

And for the first time in his life, Joshua felt like he was home.

* * * * *

Look for more books in USA TODAY *bestselling author Barb Han's miniseries* CATTLEMEN CRIME CLUB *throughout 2017.*

You'll find them wherever Harlequin Intrigue books are sold!

LARGER-PRINT
BOOKS!

HARLEQUIN *Presents®*

PASSION GUARANTEED SEDUCTION

GET 2 FREE LARGER-PRINT
NOVELS PLUS 2 FREE GIFTS!

YES! Please send me 2 FREE LARGER-PRINT Harlequin Presents® novels and my 2 FREE gifts (gifts are worth about $10). After receiving them, if I don't wish to receive any more books, I can return the shipping statement marked "cancel." If I don't cancel, I will receive 6 brand-new novels every month and be billed just $5.30 per book in the U.S. or $5.74 per book in Canada. That's a saving of at least 12% off the cover price! It's quite a bargain! Shipping and handling is just 50¢ per book in the U.S. and 75¢ per book in Canada.* I understand that accepting the 2 free books and gifts places me under no obligation to buy anything. I can always return a shipment and cancel at any time. Even if I never buy another book, the two free books and gifts are mine to keep forever.

176/376 HDN GHVY

Name _____ (PLEASE PRINT)

Address _____ Apt. #

City _____ State/Prov. _____ Zip/Postal Code

Signature (if under 18, a parent or guardian must sign)

Mail to the **Reader Service:**
IN U.S.A.: P.O. Box 1867, Buffalo, NY 14240-1867
IN CANADA: P.O. Box 609, Fort Erie, Ontario L2A 5X3

**Are you a subscriber to Harlequin Presents® books
and want to receive the larger-print edition?
Call 1-800-873-8635 today or visit us at www.ReaderService.com.**

* Terms and prices subject to change without notice. Prices do not include applicable taxes. Sales tax applicable in N.Y. Canadian residents will be charged applicable taxes. Offer not valid in Quebec. This offer is limited to one order per household. Not valid for current subscribers to Harlequin Presents Larger-Print books. All orders subject to credit approval. Credit or debit balances in a customer's account(s) may be offset by any other outstanding balance owed by or to the customer. Please allow 4 to 6 weeks for delivery. Offer available while quantities last.

Your Privacy—The Reader Service is committed to protecting your privacy. Our Privacy Policy is available online at www.ReaderService.com or upon request from the Reader Service.

We make a portion of our mailing list available to reputable third parties that offer products we believe may interest you. If you prefer that we not exchange your name with third parties, or if you wish to clarify or modify your communication preferences, please visit us at www.ReaderService.com/consumerschoice or write to us at Reader Service Preference Service, P.O. Box 9062, Buffalo, NY 14240-9062. Include your complete name and address.

HPLP15

LARGER-PRINT BOOKS!

GET 2 FREE LARGER-PRINT NOVELS PLUS
2 FREE GIFTS!

HARLEQUIN®

Romance

From the Heart, For the Heart

YES! Please send me 2 FREE LARGER-PRINT Harlequin® Romance novels and my 2 FREE gifts (gifts are worth about $10). After receiving them, if I don't wish to receive any more books, I can return the shipping statement marked "cancel." If I don't cancel, I will receive 4 brand-new novels every month and be billed just $5.09 per book in the U.S. or $5.49 per book in Canada. That's a savings of at least 15% off the cover price! It's quite a bargain! Shipping and handling is just 50¢ per book in the U.S. and 75¢ per book in Canada.* I understand that accepting the 2 free books and gifts places me under no obligation to buy anything. I can always return a shipment and cancel at any time. Even if I never buy another book, the two free books and gifts are mine to keep forever.

119/319 HDN GHWC

Name	(PLEASE PRINT)	

Address		Apt. #

City	State/Prov.	Zip/Postal Code

Signature (if under 18, a parent or guardian must sign)

Mail to the **Reader Service:**
IN U.S.A.: P.O. Box 1867, Buffalo, NY 14240-1867
IN CANADA: P.O. Box 609, Fort Erie, Ontario L2A 5X3
Want to try two free books from another line?
Call 1-800-873-8635 or visit www.ReaderService.com.

* Terms and prices subject to change without notice. Prices do not include applicable taxes. Sales tax applicable in N.Y. Canadian residents will be charged applicable taxes. Offer not valid in Quebec. This offer is limited to one order per household. Not valid for current subscribers to Harlequin Romance Larger-Print books. All orders subject to credit approval. Credit or debit balances in a customer's account(s) may be offset by any other outstanding balance owed by or to the customer. Please allow 4 to 6 weeks for delivery. Offer available while quantities last.

Your Privacy—The Reader Service is committed to protecting your privacy. Our Privacy Policy is available online at www.ReaderService.com or upon request from the Reader Service.

We make a portion of our mailing list available to reputable third parties that offer products we believe may interest you. If you prefer that we not exchange your name with third parties, or if you wish to clarify or modify your communication preferences, please visit us at www.ReaderService.com/consumerschoice or write to us at Reader Service Preference Service, P.O. Box 9062, Buffalo, NY 14240-9062. Include your complete name and address.

LARGER-PRINT BOOKS!
GET 2 FREE LARGER-PRINT NOVELS PLUS
2 FREE GIFTS!

HARLEQUIN®

super romance®

More Story...More Romance